John Henry McCoy

John Henry McCoy

by Lillie D. Chaffin

illustrated by Emanuel Schongut

The Macmillan Company, New York
Collier-Macmillan Ltd., London

1589998

For Ronald Levi and Rheda Ynele Chaffin

One

John Henry sat on the schoolhouse porch twiddling his thumbs. He was good at that. He'd had lots of practice, especially since the television burned out, and then they moved to a house without electricity. Not having electricity didn't worry him. He'd grown used to being without lots of things. He'd almost grown used to moving from the head of a hollow, a long distance on foot from any other house, right

1

smack-dab to one or two rooms in the middle of a big city where he couldn't move without bothering somebody below him or beside him or behind him. Then back to another hollow, where it was too lonesome for even a hoot owl if his father was away. Then to another town when Henry McCoy had found another job.

Move, move, move, John Henry thought. When factory work slowed down, his father always seemed to be the first person laid off. Then they would head back to the coal mining mountains of eastern Kentucky where John Henry had been born. But mining jobs were scarce and lasted only a few months, and soon the McCoys would move back to a city. In the city, his mother remembered the fresh country air, and his granny pined for a tree to sit under. She talked about the exercise and fresh vegetables a garden would give them. In the country, they remembered being able to turn a tap for water. John Henry could tell when his mother knew another move was ahead, and was trying to prepare them all for it, for she kept remembering the good points of some other place.

All the time his parents kept promising, "This time we'll put down roots." John Henry was not certain he knew what that meant, but he liked the sound of it. It sounded settled and unhurried, like a plant just standing and without seeming to try at all becoming thicker and taller and greener and having everything it needed. Yes, he would like to put down roots. But he never knew, when his father was away as he was now, at what minute Mr. Mc-Coy would drive up in an old pickup truck or in an old car with a U-Haul hitched to it and shout, "Let's go. We ought to a been started yesterday."

John Henry was tired of moving, tired of missing out on school. His father never went past second grade and Mrs. McCoy hadn't quite finished the fifth. They were always saying they wanted John Henry to get a good education so he could have a fine job, but John Henry wasn't learning much. He was going on eleven and didn't really know what grade he fitted into. When he went to a new school, the teachers would shift him about and test him, like a piece of puzzle, and before they decided where he fitted he'd be gone. He didn't like being a little past or nearly or going on something. He wanted to be something exactly and stay that way. And he wanted to have some things of his own.

When John Henry was five, the last big mine had

closed. The McCoys had been on welfare for a while and stayed put for a whole year while John Henry went to Head Start at Cow Pen Creek. He had collected stones then. The day school ended they had gone to Cleveland and his stones were too heavy to take along since the tires on the car were thin.

While he sat on the porch twiddling and resting, John Henry thought of running away from home, of not going home at all—maybe living in the school coal house or a cave or an old mine and washing in the creek whenever he had to wash. When he got to thinking that they might move again, he wanted to take off like a bird. There would be plenty of room in the sky. He would never be in the way up there or have to hush up, but he knew that was wishful thinking. He would never have wings, and even robins had to come down once in a while. If he got way-way up and way-way off and had to come down, he'd be afraid. For there would be strangers, and his mother and his granny were always warning him about speaking to strangers who might harm him. For a minute he closed his eyes and enjoyed all the things they had said strangers might offer to coax him to follow them—chocolate

4

bars or peppermint sticks or real windup play-pretty toys.

His stomach began feeling empty. Then he said aloud, "Them beans not cooked soon because I never got in enough wood, somebody's bellybutton's going to press on their backbone." Undercooked pinto beans were hard and the watery-looking soup made him ache inside, but when the beans were really done there was a river of good brown soup, enough for all of them when they filled their plates up with cornbread and poured the soup over it— mmm, brown as candy bars and better for you and nearly as good tasting. But cooking beans took a mighty lot of wood and coal!

School had let out early because it was the first day and the teacher had a lot of paper work to do. She'd been nice, even when he didn't know what grade he really belonged in. She had smiled and patted him a little and said, "That's all right. I've got all the grades, and I'll be needing a big boy like you to help with things." And she hadn't seemed angry when he didn't raise his hand to promise that he wouldn't be absent all year. She hadn't even asked why. As she walked up the aisle, she bent over and whispered just for him, smelling like the first spring wind, "That's all right. We'll do the best we can, won't we?"

At first glance, she hadn't seemed pretty, but she got prettier each time John Henry looked at her. Then she said, "There won't be any more classes till Monday. I'll be visiting as many of your homes as possible. If you know anyone who should be in Head Start, you tell them it'll begin in a month or so. See you Monday, and make a straight line to the door. Bye now."

He had stood frozen for a minute before he could take a step toward her. "Teacher?" he said and the next word hung in his throat and would not come out.

"Yes?"

"Miss Day, could I have one book to take home, please?"

"What kind of book would you like to take?"

"Any kind'll be all right."

He might have been a knot on a log the way the other students passed him. One boy bumped into him and rolled his eyes, as if he were daring John Henry to do something about it. When the others were outside, Miss Day took five whole minutes finding a book with bicycles and wagons in it. And she had smiled and said, "I hope you'll like this one."

The schoolhouse was so quiet he couldn't imagine what she was doing, and he wished he didn't have to go home and worry about moving again. He shifted a little so the floor crack would not cut into him, and he opened the book. Just then Miss Day came to the door.

"Oh, I thought I heard somebody out here. Hadn't you better go home?" she asked.

"Yes, I guess so. Good-by, Miss Day."

He decided he didn't really want to run away, and he was a little ashamed of himself. Fine job he was doing taking care of the family, he thought, as he picked up a buckeye and put it in his pocket. Then he hurried home.

Before he could get into the house his mother called, "John Henry McCoy, you better get some wood in a hurry, you want any supper."

"Teacher wanted us to tell about Head Start beginning soon," he said. "I hope Clarabell can go. You think she can?"

"We'll see about it when the time comes. Sara's already mentioned it," Mrs. McCoy said.

"I'll go," Clarabell said. She was at the corner of

7

the house making a row of mud pies and placing them on a flat rock for drying.

He changed his pants and tucked the book under the mattress. Then he went to the chip-yard and gathered a quick handful of splinters and chips. He dumped them into the paper box behind the stove and went back to look for some bigger pieces. There was only a slab of hickory. The dull, rusty ax hung in it at the first chop, and he gave up. He walked about looking for something large enough for stove wood.

"John Henry? John Henry!" his sister Sara called. "You'd better get here with some wood this minute. Loafing around."

"Not any."

"Some little fine coal then. And hurry, for goodness sake."

He scraped up a four-pound lard bucket full of coal and ran to the house with it.

"Bug dust," Sara groaned. "Put that slack coal in, and it'll explode like gunpowder. Mommy, he's got slack coal."

"Put it in a pinch at a time," Granny called from the back porch where she was putting up a wet-weather clothesline.

He stood holding the bucket while Sara spooned out coal, and he watched his mother take a sheet-wrapped board from across the tops of two chairs. She had been ironing since the fire had been built for cooking the beans.

"Here, let me do it," she told Sara. "Trying to iron with them old coal irons is like a cat eating a grindstone. I'm so tired I can hardly move, but I have to kill two birds with one stone. To think only a month ago I had that good steam electric iron."

"And it borrowed," Granny said. "And if them coal irons hadn't been here, we wouldn't be ironing at all. But I can think of a lot worse things than wearing clothes not ironed."

Mrs. McCoy lifted the bean pot and shook some coal under it. They had paid a dollar for the stove at a junkyard the day they moved here. It had one cap missing, but that was no problem, since things cooked faster when the kettle was closer to the fire. When the kettle was fitted again so that no smoke came into the room, she said, "Now, John Henry, you get out'n here and take in them herbs, case of rain. And mind you, don't crumble them. Every time they get mashed there's less to sell."

9

John Henry could smell the pennyroyal before he reached it. For two days he had pulled every twig to be found on the hills around the house and carried them in. Now they were spread out on the ground, drying in the sun. "School clothes," he had said when the sweat poured into his eyes and mouth. "You're my school clothes."

He stood thinking how silly it would sound if anyone had heard him and how funny he would look if he really wore these scratchy, smelly old weeds.

Sara called, "Poking again. That's the reason you didn't have new clothes for today."

"I don't care."

"Way you act, John Henry, is the reason Mommy said she might not let Clarabell go to Head Start."

Sara hadn't gone to Head Start, and sometimes she acted as if it were his fault that she hadn't been old enough.

"Oh, go find yourself a weed to pull or a flea to scratch," he said.

She threw a stick at him, and he didn't bother with dodging it. "You'll never make World Series," he said. To the tune of "Lazy Mary," he began singing "Lazy Sara."

10

She threw another stick as he finished the word "today." "Silly thing," she said.

He threw the stick back, aiming several feet to the right of her. "I learned a lot of songs in Head Start, and a lot of games, like Red Rover, and you know it."

"Don't have to go to Head Start to learn Red Rover. How's that ever going to help you get a job?"

He shrugged and started filling a sack with dried pennyroyal. He'd had lots of fun that year in the special room in back of the old school building on Cow Pen Creek. The Head Start teacher had laughed at his Tall Tales, let him be the caboose of the line for one whole day because he knew a purple crayon, let him pin a tail on a Halloween cat when he knew the word orange. He got stars for having clean hands and ribbons for carrying a tune. At school everything he did was fine.

But his family had thought he was wasting time. Every day they'd asked, "What'd you learn today?" They didn't think it was worthwhile to stretch high or curl up small or take long naps. They thought he should be doing the alphabet and numbers. Nothing had pleased them at home, not even when the class got real wagons and tricycles for riding, and he won a star for not bumping all day.

He'd given up trying to make them understand, but he would not give up Head Start. The long, winding road to the schoolhouse got slippery, and his mother thought it was too dangerous for him to go in the special pickup truck that came to the door for him. But John Henry had begged and cried until she let him go. He would not stay home and miss out on all the interesting things at school.

Sara threw the stick back at him. "You stop that cloud-walking and get in some water." She got the bucket and dipper and stood waiting. She did not consider water carrying "women's work."

After dipping water and filling the bucket, John Henry stooped down and drank from the spring. His nose got in the way, but the water tasted better. He decided to forget about his nose. That was the way to really enjoy things—forget whatever was in the way. He also forgot to hold his nose and was strangled for a minute.

A few inches above the spring a frog sat very still, except for the swelling out and drawing in of its throat. He took it up gently and looked at the little knobs of skin on its back, ran his finger over them.

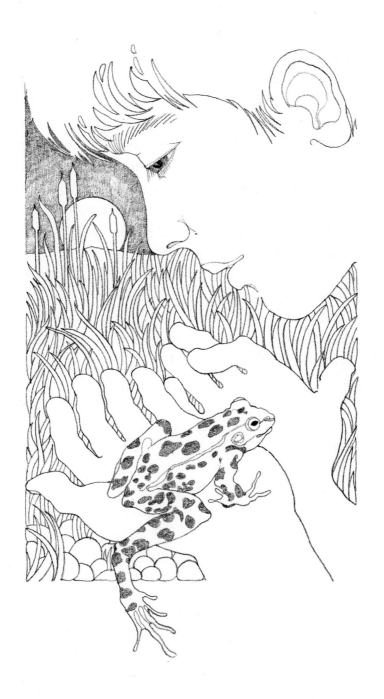

He put the frog in his pocket, and it lay there, soft, warm, a wiggling lump.

"Water," his mother called. "Water, John Henry, this minute."

He wanted to keep the frog, but it was kicking now. It wouldn't want to be fastened up in his pocket or a glass jar any more than he wanted to be fastened up away from the good warm earth under his feet. Gently he lifted it out of his pocket and set it back where it had been.

"I'm coming," he answered, running, slopping water on his pants. It was hard, at times, trying to be the man of the house. All these womenfolk needed a strong man, and he had promised his father he would take care of things.

Two

The next morning Mrs. McCoy ran her fingers across the pennyroyal in the sacks and decided it was dry enough for taking to the store.

"But you'll have to wait for the dew to dry," she said. "Don't want to get it wet, and it'll be too heavy to carry all the way."

"Let me go and help," Sara begged. She was always ready to go anywhere at any time.

"Teacher might come up," John Henry said, but

15

he didn't really expect her. It was a long walk from the school.

"Me go too," Clarabell said, wiping sleep from her big brown eyes.

"Mommy's baby can't go off and leave her. Boogerman might get Mommy if you go off. I thought I heard something last night, tramping around the house. You two don't go telling the man down there that your daddy went into town for our groceries while he was here. Some people don't want your trade if they can't get it all," Mrs. McCoy said.

Sara finished combing her hair. She slept so soundly hardly any noise could wake her. "Did you really hear something?" she asked.

Clarabell puckered to cry. "Granny won't let a boogerman get you, will you, Granny? I never get to go nowhere."

Not wanting to take sides, Granny pretended not to hear.

John Henry couldn't understand why they all wanted to be on the go. Hattie, Mattie, and Marylou, his three older sisters, had married, one in Detroit, one in Chicago and one in Akron, and they kept busy moving and going to see each other. They all talked about getting ahead, acting as if "ahead"

16

was somewhere they had to run after. They planned over and over that they'd save money, buy a house, buy furniture—always on the next job. But they kept paying rent and paying on secondhand things and running to other towns, looking for the end of a rainbow.

Today, though, John Henry was really eager to go to the store. Somehow, it seemed, if he had the cloth for making shirts for school, it would mean he was really going to put down roots.

When Sara had on her yesterday's dress, they started down the hollow. She was quiet until she stumped her toe. Then he had to wait for her to decide to stop dancing about and go ahead.

The creek wound about the hollow-road, and they had to cross it four times. Each time, John Henry waded over and over and over with a sack on his back. Once they bent over and watched silver-sided minnows weave up and down the shallow water and slide under the edges of the rocks they used for stepping stones. Sara had to say, "Come on, John Henry, if you plan to get there and back today."

They cracked some green-tasting black walnuts and made a pile of them to take home later. Again Sara said, "Come on, John Henry." They found a

17

turtle on its back, where it had fallen over a cliff, and John Henry turned it over. Someone had left a fire on the bank where the creek was deep, and John Henry threw sand on the fire. He caught a golden maple leaf which sailed out before him, and he laid the bags on the ground and began searching for a leaf without holes in it. He saw a spider building a web and a crawdad digging a well and a grasshopper jumping. Each time Sara said, "Come on, John Henry." Everything was as new as if he had not gone by it twice yesterday, as if he had never been in the country before.

"You know something, it's funny how a spider and things like that're so fine out in the open, and a bug in a city apartment's about the worst thing. Gives folks the chills and then the scrubs, doesn't it? Got'cha!" he shouted and dropped a leaf on Sara's head, expecting her to scream and start running.

Instead, she rammed a finger into his ribs and shouted, "Got you!" When he jumped, she laughed. "If it won't hurt you, it won't hurt me. Granny told me that."

Far back from the road there was a house with its windows boarded up. An apple tree with loaded limbs hung over an old rail fence. "Let's make a pile to take home," he said.

"May belong to somebody," Sara said.

"They can't use them all, and they won't care."

"This is the longest hollow we ever lived in. And nobody else in it. Why'd people ever build so far apart?"

"Because they wanted to." Then John Henry explained a little more. He liked talking to Sara when she was in the mood for listening. "The teacher in Akron told us about the pioneers. They liked the wild life, plant and animal. You remember there's a poem about Daniel Boone saying over and over, 'Elbow room.' And if you had fifty or a hundred or a thousand acres, you built a house as near the middle as you could find a good spot."

At the mouth of the hollow, the big road lay thick with dust and uneven with last winter's ruts. Thompson's Drink Pepsi Grocery sat on the edge of the mountain-cut road with its back on stilts and a little room under it built of cinder blocks. There was hardly room between the storefront and the road for the wooden crates of bottles, the pile of tin cans, and the rusting refrigerators and parts of old cars.

19

Hezzy Thompson was sitting on a bale of hay beside the store. He was peeling an apple, not seeming to mind the two yellowjackets that circled the apple and the knife.

"Big crop of yellowjackets means a bad winter," he said. "What can I do for you younguns?"

"Some herbs to trade," Sara said, as if he could not see the sacks, and as if they belonged to her.

He looked at the bags a little sadly and shook his head. "About stocked up on herbs. Price down. And it costs me a little more every trip I have to make to get them into town for selling. You're sure they're dry through and through? Damp inside, they're heavy and they rot. Bring them in."

John Henry wiped his sweaty face on his shirttail first.

Inside, the building was so dark after the bright sunlight outside that John Henry stepped on a broom handle and nearly fell. Mr. Thompson dumped the contents of one sack onto a piece of canvas on the floor, felt over the leaves and stems and threw a handful of stems onto the floor.

"Not hardly dry as they might a been." He set a sack on a scale. "H'm, have to dock you a little." He searched under a pile of papers, patted his shirt pockets, then patted his pants pockets and came up with a small and well-chewed pencil. "Dollar and a half. You're the folks I heard had moved to the head of Hatfield Branch?"

"That's right," Sara said. She was going up and down the shelves with her eyes, pricing things, wanting them.

"Cat got your tongue, boy?" The man rubbed his mouth, fingered his upper lip and measured a week's growth of beard.

"No sir. You just weighed one sack."

"Same size sacks weigh the same thing, unless you weight them down with rocks or something. I can about look at a sack and tell what should be in it, give or take a pound or so." Mr. Thompson nodded and waited.

"I'd like to see some shirt cloth," John Henry said.

"Don't know as I've heard what you-all's name is. What is it, and where you from, and where you been trading?"

John Henry left Sara to answer while he looked over a hammer and an ax. Once, in Cleveland, they had lived near a hardware store, and he had wanted a hammer so badly he had carried one home. His

21

father made him take it back and apologize. The storekeeper had let him dust shelves to pay for it, and he still had it. The old ax he had been using belonged with the house. A new ax might split some of that tough hickory. He ran his finger along the shiny edge. It would need sharpening first, and he couldn't sharpen an ax. His father could, though. Henry McCoy, when he set his hand to it, could sharpen an ax so that it would sink into wood as if the wood were butter.

"What'd you say your name was again? Mine's Thompson, as you probably saw on the sign out front." Sara told him their names, and he scratched his head and figured on a piece of brown wrapping paper.

Mr. Thompson spread both hands on the counter and leaned forward. "For somebody worth the salt goes in their bread, I've got a good deal. First, I'd like to get some fence posts cut. You tell your daddy that, will you? When'd you expect him back? Where's he at?"

Sara was tired, and she nodded at John Henry. John Henry said, "He's looking for work somewhere, or working somewhere."

"You mean he just up and left you-all?" When

John Henry shook his head, the man continued, "Well, it's good to know you've not been left. Seems like he was here and asked for work, but I didn't have anything just then. Got a deal on locust fence posts later."

John Henry bent over the two bolts of cloth Mr. Thompson thumped onto the counter. Let Sara talk. Granny always said Sara's tongue was tied in the middle and loose at both ends, and like a brook, she ran on forever. And Granny said, "It's like pulling a hangnail, at times, to get a word out of John Henry."

He pulled up a layer of cloth on one bolt and then on the other while Sara said, "See, Daddy's either got a job or he's still looking. He goes from one town to another till he finds work. He always finds a job. He's not been gone long enough for us to hear yet, I guess. When he gets a job, he'll come after us."

"Here today and gone tomorrow, huh?" Mr. Thompson asked.

John Henry knew it was an awful thing to wish, but he wished his father wouldn't find a job. Then they could put down roots here, could gather berries in the summer and pawpaws and roots and leaves for using and for selling. They could plant a garden and maybe raise a cow, and collect things. Then he could go all year, year after year, to the same school, and stop being a stranger.

"I can say." Mr. Thompson was shaking his head as he spoke. "You sure can go off somewhere. I can let you have three yards of either piece of this cloth you want. That'll make two shirts for a boy your size, and be a little left over."

John Henry hadn't really been paying much attention to the cloth. "What do you think, Sara?" he asked.

She rubbed dust from a package of bobby pins. "For a dress or a shirt?" she teased.

"You got dresses. They always send you dresses."

"Who's they?" Mr. Thompson asked.

"They" were the older sisters who could buy used dresses for nearly nothing, but shirts and pants, they said, were hard to find because boys were rough on their clothes. Sara started explaining, but when a tall fat woman came with a basket of eggs for trading, Mr. Thompson lost interest in Sara's story. "You make up your mind while I wait on her. Howdy, Lidie. How're you-all today?"

"Will's kind a poorly, but the rest of us're about

so-so. Younguns up in the air about school and all."

"This'd make the prettiest shirt." Sara laid her fingers on the brown cloth and let them slide back and forth.

John Henry had thought the blue striped was prettiest, and they wondered if they should get half and half. Two pieces might not be enough for making anything, and blue would show soil easier, so they decided on the brown. When the choice was made, there was nothing to do but wait for the woman to decide between one piece of fat salt bacon and another, between rice and oatmeal, and between self-rising meal and plain.

"I never seem to have all the stuff to put in bread. Give me that fancy kind," she said. She chose the fat back meat without a stripe of lean. "Lean's like brine, and tough," she said. And she chose rice "because it swells up and fills you up."

When the woman had gone, Mr. Thompson unrolled the cloth, stretched it from one notch on the counter to another three times, gave a little snip with some rusty scissors which had one point missing. Then he tore it, and John Henry stood wondering if that one frayed inch might mean the loss of a shirt for him.

When the cloth was in the brown paper on which Mr. Thompson had been figuring, John Henry said, "I'd like to have some bobby pins for Sara, if there's enough left over to pay for them. If there's not enough, you can charge them to me, and I'll pay you soon as I can."

Mr. Thompson gave Sara the bobby pins, then reached behind the counter and brought out two cellophane-wrapped orange suckers. "Now, that'll about square us. You bring any more suckers—I mean any more herbs—see that you pick out all the big stalks, sonny. And you-all can tell your pa I'd like to see him. Might be my old woman'd have some work for your womenfolks too, if they can do any housework at all. Well?"

It did not appear that they were going to get their bags back, and John Henry said, "May we please have our sacks? They're all we got."

"I'll get you some." The man kicked three sacks from the corner toward them. "And you-all don't take no six-cent pieces."

Sara carried the package and the bobby pins, and John Henry carried the sacks, and they wished he had given them different-flavored suckers so they could have traded licks on them.

When they reached the apple tree, they scooped apples into a sack. They lifted the sack, and apples fell out a hole in the bottom. The second sack had two holes pinned with nails. The third one had several holes near the top, but they put some apples in it, and John Henry carried them. A big dog, black and white speckled and bony, was lying near the fishing hole. He got up, wagged his tail. John Henry patted him, and he curved like a rainbow. "Good dog, Fido," John Henry said.

"How'd you know his name's Fido?" Sara asked as she shifted the package to the other hand and patted the dog.

"I don't. That's what I'd call him. Come on, Fido. We'll come back and get us some more apples if Mommy'll let us."

The dog followed for a while, then turned back.

Granny was sitting on the edge of the porch, sewing a crazy-quilt patch from the best pieces of a coat Clarabell had outgrown. The ends of her fingers were covered with little holes where she had jabbed them with the needle.

"I forgot to tell you to try to spare me enough from the herb money for a new thimble," she said. "Mmm, them smells good." She took an apple, wiped it on her skirt and bit into it. "Rome Beauty's the best apple on earth. Had enough, we'd dry some. Had sugar, we could fry us a skillet full and make some pies and dumplings and some sauce and some cake. And apple butter. Apples are good for everything. I sure am glad you brought them. Now I'd better get to work on your shirts. Want to backstitch the seams and that's more time but better. Sara, see if you can find an old shirt and get me some buttons, and I'll get this all measured up." Then Granny saw the holes in the sacks. " 'Pon my word, next time you trade something, you tell that man we can't carry things in sacks that ragged. We lost on that part of the deal."

Granny spread the cloth on the bed. Then she measured John Henry's arms with a piece of string and hung it across the end of the tin bedpost. She measured his shoulders and laid the string across the pillows. She measured and measured and then took an old shirt and estimated how much bigger the new one needed to be.

"Better come and get a bite," Mrs. McCoy said. "Then, John Henry, I'd like you and Sara to go up the hill and drag in some wood. Time you learned hickory won't split and oak won't hardly and chestnut pops too much. Poplar's good. I was going to tell you to be looking and see if there's a coal seam along the way to the store. Pick us up some good cooking coal. Could even use a pick, if we had one, around the edges and gouge us out some for bean and ironing and washing days. I sure do miss that nice gas stove we had up there in Cleveland."

"Gas's too mean to blow up. Afraid of it," Granny said.

Sara frowned. "We wanted to go back and get some more apples. Some walnuts. Dry some, Granny said."

Mrs. McCoy trotted her feet. "Last dried apples we made got bugs in them, and they molded too."

"Because we moved before they dried, Mary, and hardly a mess of them anyway," Granny said.

Sara began, "Mr. Thompson said to tell Daddy—"

"Daddy's gone," Clarabell interrupted.

"Goofy, I know it. He said to tell Daddy that he had some fence posts needed cutting, that he might have some work for you and Granny, Mommy."

"And you don't call people names, little girl. It's not nice. I'll tell your daddy, and we'll see about it as soon as we can."

By the time Sara and John Henry had dragged

29

down a long tree limb and chopped it for stove wood, it was getting late. Granny had sewn only two seams on one shirt, but no one could have told from the top side that the seams were done by hand. After a supper of meal gravy and sauerkraut, they went outside. John Henry helped Clarabell and Sara chase lightning bugs and put them in a jar. When night had crept all the way down the hill, and they were too hot and tired to move, they sat on the porch. Clarabell sat in Mrs. McCoy's lap; Sara leaned on Granny. John Henry went off to the end of the porch where there was plenty of room for twiddling his thumbs and for petting the dog that had walked up so quietly no one else had heard him. Fido. Yes, he would name the dog Fido. Fido thumped his tail against the wall.

"What's that?" Mrs. McCoy asked.

"Let's sing awhile. Some good old songs," John Henry said.

Granny began in her high cracked voice: "I'm a poor wayfaring stranger." The others joined in. "Traveling in this land below." John Henry stopped there. He did not want to be a stranger, and he was tired of traveling.

When the song ended, his mother said, "John

31

Henry, would you stop that banging on the wall? It gets on my nerves. Sounds a little like the noise I heard last night. Prowler maybe. And if I hear it again tonight, I'm going to do something. Maybe get that old gun out and use it."

"Might be a groundhog or possum, or something," John Henry said, "and don't you go to thinking about using a gun, Mommy, please." The McCoy family was never without a gun. It made Mr. McCoy feel that his family was safe. Mrs. McCoy had never shot it even in practice, because shells were costly and not to be wasted. Still, the thought of her shooting at Fido scared him, and John Henry said again, "Might be a groundhog or possum."

"Then we just may have some wild meat—if Mary can find the shells and aim straight," Granny said.

"Might be somebody," John Henry said. He was holding the thumpety tail, which was now like a steel rod as the dog tried to get away. He turned the tail loose and it eased into a curve and started whacking the wall again.

"If it's somebody, a little buckshot nearby might teach them a lesson."

32

"No, Mommy, it might be a pony," Sara said. "A pony could get loose. I've wanted a pony all my born days."

"Or something else good and fine," John Henry said. "Something like a dog maybe. Maybe a hunting dog or a watchdog."

"We had a fine watchdog once, Mary, remember?" Granny's voice got soft, as it always did when she talked about that first Fido they'd had. "For a whole year we had that dog, and it was like pulling a tooth to give him away, but Henry got that job at the car factory and that was that."

"What if we did have a dog, Mommy?" The dog licked John Henry's hand, and his tongue was warm and friendly. "Why don't we, why can't we? To watch and hunt, and, oh, to play with sometimes?"

"We can't feed a dog, and you know it," Mrs. McCoy said. "That's enough, and it's bedtime. I better send you-all to the post office tomorrow, and see if there's a letter from your daddy. Now, let's all get some sleep."

"If we had a good dog, and we had to go away for just a little while, couldn't we loan him out and get him back?" John Henry sighed. He was not certain he was making himself clear.

33

"Reckon what Henry's doing now? I sure do miss that boy," Granny said.

Sara laughed. "You talk like Daddy's a youngun. I know what I wish—that he could stay here or us all go there and stay with him."

Granny carried her chair inside. "That's what we all wish. And, Sara, he'll never get too big or too old to be my baby. I remember my own ma calling me a baby."

John Henry had never thought of Granny as being anybody's baby. Somehow it had seemed the world began with Granny. He pushed the dog a little, guided him under the porch. He knelt and patted Fido and whispered, "Stay, now you stay right here," and then eased away.

"If you don't get in here I'm going to lock you out," his mother called.

"And I will too," Granny added.

He went in immediately, but he did not once believe they would lock him out. It was his mother's way of saying "now you mind me this minute" and her way of saying "I have to take care of everyone now that Daddy's away." It was Granny's way of saying "I'm with you, Mary" and "I love you, John Henry." They didn't say "I love you" in those exact

34

words very often, but they said it, and they all understood that it was being said.

He thought for a while before he fell asleep. Maybe they talked tough to hide the tender feelings. Maybe they talked big because most of what they did for each other was not as big as they would have liked it to be. When they lived in a city, Granny said, "We stay on the road, and I'm wore out with it," or "We move every time the wind changes, and I'm going to put my foot down one of these days and refuse to budge again." She always budged, after a while, and none of them ever believed any of these stops was that permanent. When "back home," to the country, was the direction of moving, she even grumbled a little about leaving some good neighbor who shared their apartment building. Mr. McCoy always understood and said, "You have to take what these womenfolks around here say with a grain of salt."   **1589998**

John Henry wished his father could be with them. He had tried for two weeks to find work after they moved to Hatfield Branch. "It's not much use to earn a living," he had said, "if you can't live it with your family." The finest house in the world would be a little empty if his father were not there.

35

Three

Granny and Sara slept in one bed. Mrs. McCoy and Clarabell slept at the head of the other bed, and John Henry slept at the foot of it. He felt under the mattress, and the book was there, warm and good, like a turkey in the oven on Thanksgiving morning. He planned to read the book as soon as there was time to do so. Under the floor, Fido thumped, and John Henry turned to cover the

36

sound. If his mother had a little time, she would get used to the idea of having a dog.

"John Henry, if you don't be still I'm going to make you sleep on the floor," his mother scolded when he turned for the tenth time.

He'd slept on the floor lots of times when all the family was home. Sleeping on it now wouldn't bother him, except that if he stayed in bed he might be able to cover up for Fido's noises.

The window was gray with daylight when he awoke the next morning. He listened as Granny gave her long breath, short breath, long breath, short breath, and it was so peaceful he became drowsy. Then he thought of Fido. He would go hunting with Fido, and they would bring back a groundhog or a possum, and his mother would see they needed the dog. The more he thought about it the more excited he became. They would catch so many animals they could sell them. Granny had said she loved groundhog, and if Fido helped her have groundhog, she wouldn't let Fido go.

John Henry moved an inch at a time toward the side of the bed. Every move squeaked or jiggled something. When his toes were over the edge, he shifted his hips an inch up and over, then another inch and another. When his feet were on the floor, he took his pants from the bedpost and tiptoed, thump, squeak, thump, squeak, to the kitchen. He took a square of cornbread from the tin pan on the back of the stove. Scooting his feet made a little less noise, so he scooted to the door.

When he was on the cool, damp ground, he slipped into his pants. He had expected Fido to be there waiting. "Here, Fido. Here, doggie," he whispered. Somewhere a cricket sang a quiet hymn to morning. A bird chirp sounded to John Henry like "sweet, sweet." A poplar leaf fell at his feet, a golden butter-yellow in the center and ragged brown at the tip, and when he reached for the leaf, as a kind of good luck charm, he found a three-cornered stone—maybe an Indian arrowhead. He brushed the dampness from it and dropped it in his pocket.

John Henry eased around the house. The dog was not under the porch, not on it. "Here, Fido. Here, good doggie," he called a little louder, but there was no answer. He sat down for a minute to wait and to think. He was hungry, and he broke the bread carefully in half and ate his share of it. He put the other piece in his pocket and walked around the house on tiptoe.

He climbed the hill to a mulberry tree and stood calling a little louder. Granny had talked of eating fresh mulberries, of mulberry pie, but he had never eaten a mulberry. One year they had lived near a mulberry tree, and he had watched the berries turn from plain, thin, greenish worm-looking to a plump red. Before the red could change to the purplish black of ripeness, the McCoys had moved to Chicago.

His pants caught on a blackberry vine. Last year they had picked a few blackberries. He had never tasted anything so good in all his life. He kicked the bare, no-good, sticky briar now. A persimmon plopped on his foot and rolled a few inches away. The day after they had moved here, he and his father came up this way, and his father located the tree: "When persimmons are ripe—" John Henry dusted the persimmon on his knee and stuck it in his mouth. One tooth bit through the slick skin, and his mouth dried up. Before he could spit it out, his mouth grew small and rough. Turned wrong side out, it seemed. To be rid of the taste, he took a pinch of bread and held it until the bread had sweetened his tongue again. Then he remembered the rest of the sentence had been, "—is right after a big frost."

39

"Fido, here. Here, Fido," he called louder now.

Above him there was a thump. A hickory nut hit a tree branch, balanced for a minute, then fell. The tree had bushels and bushels of the long, hard nuts. John Henry took up a rock and hammered at one. At last it broke open. The meat was small but very sweet.

"Ee." The sound came above the hammering. "John Hen-ree?"

"Coming," he shouted back.

"What in the world do you mean scaring me like that?" his mother asked when he was there and breathless from running. Before he could answer, she went on, "You answer me when I call. Don't you know better than to scare me like that?"

"I wasn't scaring you. I was looking around, for groundhogs and things. Big hickory nut tree up there."

"Why don't you get us up some good hickory nuts?" Granny asked. "They're harder'n the dickens to crack, but awful good in candy and popcorn."

His mother had not given up. She took him by the shoulders and shook him a little with a kind of hug included in it. "Bed empty and I couldn't imagine. Then I thought you might a got snakebit out somewhere. Miles away from a doctor. Why'd you do it?"

John Henry took out the arrowhead and polished it before laying it on the window sill beside Granny's thimble and thread and Clarabell's corncob doll. "I just did," he said.

"I've a notion of us going down there and getting us some more of them apples," Granny said. "We'll have sugar some time. Nothing better under the sun than apple pie with nuts. When I was a girl . . ."

Granny could talk for hours about the wonderful things that had been everyday happenings long ago. Then people were neighbors for miles and miles around, and they made work into a party. There were apple peelings and berry pickings, nut gatherings and corn huskings. The men traded dogs and horses and knives, and the women traded recipes and patterns, while the children romped through dozens of games, and the young girls and young men got interested in each other. When Granny got started on molasses-making, John Henry could smell the rich steam rising from the pans of cane juice and taste the thick golden foam on his tongue. If they had a farm, they could make all those things happen again.

41

They were always too early for one thing and too late for another. Too late to plant a crop. Too early for pawpaws and persimmons and grapes and berries.

"I know I heard something out there last night," Mrs. McCoy said. "Didn't sound like a person."

"We saw a dog down at the old house," Sara said. "Might could a been that dog, Mommy."

To change the subject, John Henry said quickly, "You know Miss Clay told us not to say might could."

Sara stuck out her tongue. "Miss Clay's not here, and I can say what I good and well like. Is there anything wrong with might could, Mommy?"

"Not that I know of. So's people understand what you're saying's all that matters to me, and you younguns better not go around that house. Wonder who it belongs to?" The answer did not really matter, and Mrs. McCoy said, "First, I'm going to let you and John Henry go to the post office. Could take a sack and bring us back some nuts or apples."

When John Henry and Sara reached the biggest curve, where the slate rock crumbled onto the side of the road, they stopped to cool in the shade of a great white-trunked sycamore. Sara plucked a piece of fern and tucked it in her hair, like a giant feather.

She put her hand over her mouth and cried, "Woo-ooo." She pointed to the large clumps of quivering ferns. "You ever see so many ferns?"

"One time, when we lived at Dry Fork for a while. Bridge washed out, and we had to use a neighbor's boat to get to the store. That was a good place, if we hadn't been there during the wet spell."

Sara laughed at John Henry's attempt to keep a fern on his head. "You like it here, don't you?" When he nodded, she asked, "Why? I get so lonesome."

"Oh, I just do. Trees and rocks and everything. And we'll get acquainted with people before long, make us some friends." He shrugged and lost the fern he had tucked into a buttonhole.

"Sometimes I think I like town better. The picture shows and all. But you like the country better, don't you?"

"I guess so. Dirt under your feet. Space all around. And we can gather up things and make collections. Remember the rock collection we made at Dry Branch, and then had to leave it?" He had been tossing the larger pieces of slate at a willow tree with its roots hanging into the water like giant

43

fingers. "We might could find us some good rocks and start again."

"There, you said it now, smarty." Sara started running. "Come on, John Henry."

He caught her when she stepped too heavily in blue mud, and he thumped her on the back. "Said what?"

"Might could."

They hung the sacks on a fence post to keep them dry, and the sacks fell. "I'll take them to the porch so nobody'll get them," John Henry said. He didn't expect anyone to bother the sacks. He wanted to do some exploring. "And you don't have to go and tell. I'm not going to bother anything."

"I'm going too," Sara said.

They waded through knee-high goldenrod, waist-high ironweed and head-high horseweeds, then walked under a row of small trees. Closer to it, they could see the house had once been white. Now the front porch sagged, boards had been nailed over windows where the panes were missing and birds were flying in and out of the upstairs window where the boards were loose. "Wow," John Henry said when he saw how big the house was. "Gee, look at that," Sara said, looking up at the birds. Back of the house, they could see acres and acres of flat land that was grown up in bushes and weeds.

"Who'd go off and leave a fine place like this?" Sara wondered. "If I had this, I'd live upstairs."

"If I had all this land, I'd raise popcorn and molasses and—and everything," John Henry said.

When they reached the store, Mr. Thompson was sitting on a bale of hay. "You look more like hayseeds today than city slickers," he said. When they didn't seem to understand, he said, "Look at your clothes."

Little, flat, sticktight burrs covered the legs of John Henry's pants and the skirt of Sara's dress.

"Where you-all headed?" he asked.

"Post office," Sara told him, "and we don't even know where it is."

"You've come to the right place. This is it, the May Post Office, named for my mother who started it. No mail, though. I'd a remembered. How's things up your way? Pa not come in yet, I reckon?"

Sara was too busy counting yellowjackets in a case of Pepsi Cola bottles to answer, and John Henry shook his head.

"Bet you had molasses for breakfast and glued your tongue down. How's the old house?" Mr.

Thompson reached into his pocket and came out with a knife and a piece of wood which dangled strangely.

Sara saw the wood and ran to look at it more closely. John Henry bent over to examine it. It was two links of a chain fastened together, and Mr. Thompson had started on the third and fourth links.

"Oh, that's pretty," Sara said. "What's it for?"

"A layover to catch meddlers. No, just a way of passing time between trades."

"What'll you do with it when it's finished?" Sara asked.

"Give it to you if you're still around and want it. I've made a heap of them, the last few years. Pity I can't sell my whittling. Soon as folks get cars, they start spending their cash in town, bring me their credit. I asked about my old house up there, the one you pass." He scraped a rough corner on the wood.

"Is that really yours?" Sara asked, her eyes sparkling as she touched a link of the chain. "Why don't you live in it? It's pretty."

"Used to live there, before I started the store business. Been five years since anybody lived in it. For ten years before that just drifters, in and out,

47

a week or a month, break out window glass and chop down fences. Your pa comes in, tell him I'd like to see him."

"You care if we get some apples up there?" Sara asked.

A fat man with a red face got out of a gray jeep, and Mr. Thompson called, "Know anybody wants to buy some apples, Andy?"

The man loosened his sweaty shirt where it was plastered to his back and answered, "Not a soul. Everybody's got more apples this year than they know what to do with."

"Help yourself, just so you don't damage my trees," Mr. Thompson said, nodding at Sara. He whetted his knife on a stone. "Got a real good knife yesterday from Tom Jinks, Andy. Want to swap?"

John Henry wanted to stay and watch the knife swapping, but Sara said, "Thanks, Mr. Thompson. John Henry, we better go."

John Henry remembered the book, and he remembered Fido. Maybe Fido was Mr. Thompson's dog, or he might know something about him. He opened his mouth to ask, but Sara shook her head and said, "Come on now."

When they reached the old house, they walked around it, a little sad that such a fine house had been left empty for so long.

"It's not seeming right, us not got anything, does it—is it?" Sara asked. "I mean, him and us, and all."

There was the sound of an engine, and they dashed to the corner of the house. "Down the road, I guess, but it sounded close," John Henry said. "I tell you what. I'm going to have a house of my own someday, and I'm not going to leave it, and I'm going to put me down some roots there." He remembered the candy Mr. Thompson had under a glass case. "And I just may have me a store too."

A giant blacksnake slithered ahead of them, like a fat ribbon, and Sara screamed.

"Aw, it won't hurt you. Blacksnakes eat mice and stuff. Scaredy, boo boo," he teased.

"I'm not taking chances. By the time you know what color one is, it could be too late. I'm going home right now, you're going to make fun of me!"

"You wait and help me with these apples. You wait!" he shouted.

Sara stuck out her tongue, waved and ran up the hollow. John Henry dropped apples into one sack, then crammed the other sack on top of it. He found

49

a piece of tin, set the apples on it to save the bottom of the sack, and dragged it a bit over stones, slid it through the creek, careful to keep the holey side up.

There was a car at the gate, a faded blue car with cardboard in the back window and a piece of plastic over the left front window. The back wheels were scotched with rocks and the front ones with blocks of wood. The flash of gladness John Henry felt was gone almost as soon as it began. When Henry McCoy came home, they moved. When they moved, their roots came up. From country to city, from space and creek and hill and rock to concrete and crowded buildings.

John Henry took the extra sack and eased away. "Here, Fido. Here, doggie," he called. But there was no answer. A squirrel, its tail curled like a question mark, hurried away. He pinned holes with a stick and filled the sack with hickory nuts from a tree across the creek. He watched an ant carrying away nut crumbs from the ones he had cracked earlier. He wished he could follow the ant, go down into its hole and live there.

He fastened the top of the sack with a nail and rolled it down the hill. He could hear voices inside the house, but he did not want to hear the words, not yet, not now. He emptied the walnuts and went down the hollow again. He sat under a tree and ate a large apple. If he knew where the teacher lived, he would go and live with her. But she wouldn't want him. Why should she care? Maybe he could tell his father how he felt.

Sara met him when he started home. "Shame on you. Where you been loafing?" she scolded.

"Nowhere."

"Daddy's home and you know it, and you didn't even come in."

John Henry kicked the sack. Sweat rolled down his cheeks. Sara could see the sweat and the load. Why did people ask such stupid questions? She was a little too happy to suit him. "It's your fault. You was supposed to be helping me," he shouted. She rolled her eyes and shrugged her shoulders to deny any blame. "What's he want?" John Henry growled.

"What a crazy question. And you can't guess in a month of Sundays what he promised me."

"The moon." John Henry had to deny her right to any promises. She hadn't done a thing to help, and he would tell on her if she kept acting so high and mighty. "The moon with a gold ring around it." He had heard lots of promises. Granny said at times

51

that promises were like pie crusts: easily broken. Not that his dad meant to tell a fib. Henry McCoy made plans and made promises, but the job always shut down or he got fired or laid off and they were asked to move because they couldn't pay rent and were too noisy—always something before the promises came true.

"I'm going to tell on you for acting smart," Sara said.

"Tell and see who gives a big rat hole."

Mr. McCoy came out on the porch, and John Henry forgot that he was sad and worried. He forgot rock collections and dogs, berries and parties. He left the sack of apples in the yard and ran. He hugged his dad two or three times, squeezing his fingers into the broad back and rubbing his smooth cheek against the rough one.

"Let me look at you." Mr. McCoy pushed him away and nodded. "Swear I believe you've shot up an inch taller, and me not been gone two weeks. They say you're really working. Getting tanned too. But we can't haul all these apples. Do well to get us all in that car, come tomorrow."

"What's Mommy and Granny say?" John Henry choked out.

Granny blocked the doorway as they started through it. "I, for one, say no. These younguns are better off here, old'ns too."

Mr. McCoy made fists and jabbed to each side of her playfully as he said, "Now, Ma, you don't mean all that."

"Every word of it. You may be too big for me to spank with a switch, but not with my tongue. I'm tired of moving, and I'm in no mind to be pinned up in a city. Matter of fact, I'm clean tired and wore out with picking up and taking off every time the moon changes. When we left Detroit, we left our radio to pay on rent, and our good iron to boot, and we left my own mother's egg basket and my trunk in Chicago. Every time we go, we leave something either because we don't have room or to pay on rent. Cram people into that little bitty car and leave all my quilts and my wash kettle your own pa bought me? I won't do it."

"Now, Ma." He put his arm around her thin shoulders. "A good puff of wind'd blow you away, and you think you're big enough to sass me?" he teased.

"Might not be much to leave, but it's all we got. Can't pay anybody to store it, and you know finder's keepers. How'd you know that job'd last a month? I think we ought to vote on it. How many say they want to go to Columbus, Ohio, tomorrow?"

Sara's hand went up, and she added to it, "I do."

John Henry watched his mother. She rarely voted on anything. Once she had explained that it was her job to take care of the family wherever they lived, that first of all Henry was the boss, which was the way a family had to be. What everybody else said had to come second, and whatever they said counted only if Henry agreed. If they didn't move now, it wouldn't be the first time they had held out for a while. But much as she disliked moving, she disliked it even more when they were not all together, and there was nothing to hold her in one place.

"I want to do what's right by everybody," she said at last.

John Henry said, "I've got a book belongs to the teacher, and I'll have to take it back, and I only went one day, but it's a good school."

"They've got good schools up there and good teachers, and I'll buy you a book. Promised a new dress to my girl babies already." When John Henry dropped his head, Mr. McCoy said, "Son?" John

54

Henry kept his head down. He put his hand in his pocket and rubbed the buckeye. "Look, I can't see why you-all've got so taken up with this old shack. Miles from nowhere. Have to wade snow knee deep all winter. Flood waters come spring. I guess nobody gives a hoot about me any more."

He took Clarabell on his knee and sat down on the lower end of the porch. Mrs. McCoy sat down beside him and put her hand in his. "Henry, if we take off now, we'll have to leave everything we own."

"I tried to keep the pickup, Mary. Motor went out, and it would a cost more to fix it than it was worth, and I traded even. We can get us a place ready-furnished."

Granny had not left the door. She said, "You mean you don't have one?"

"I've always taken care of you-all, and you know it. Got no right to complain." He got up and walked back and forth across the porch, his hands in his pockets, his head bent and worried.

John Henry wanted to comfort his father, without committing himself to moving. "You're a good daddy at taking care of us," he said.

"No reason why we can't wait a spell," Granny said. "We've waited before. You're close enough to come home every week or two from Columbus, Henry. You take a minute and think it over, and you'll see."

"I can see already. But I worry too much about you-all here, so far away from things. Be snow before you know it."

"Let's wade that snow when we get to it. Man down at the store's got them posts, might have more work." Granny wrapped her hands in her apron and waited.

"You know I can't quit a job for two or three days cutting timber. Younguns got three miles to walk a day, and you're all disturbed about them leaving that school."

"Good exercise, if we had boots," John Henry said. "I find things walking, things to keep, like shells and rocks." He curled his toes over the edge of the porch and, not waiting for a scolding for talking out of turn, jumped down. Ramming his hands in his pockets, he ran off to find some dry wood. There was another buckeye in his path, and he picked it up, polished it on his pants, and dropped it into his pocket.

He could tell by the tone of voice how much his father hated leaving them, and he had almost said,

"Why don't you stay?" But a man had to work. Henry McCoy could accept that question from the women, but not from John Henry. He expected John Henry to understand this kind of thing.

At first he thought it was a turtle lying against a mossy stump. He eased toward it, hoping it would not be frightened and fasten itself away from him. He touched the shell, and it flopped over, empty. He picked it up and ran his fingers across the smooth orange and brown squares, over the rough lines between them. He laid it on the porch before going on to the creek bank for the wood he had located earlier.

Darkness settled over the hollow, and with it came the night sounds. Frogs called. Wings slid above them. A crow cawed. John Henry waited for Fido, but the dog did not come.

Four

John Henry meant to go looking for the dog the next morning, but he slept late. At breakfast, Mr. McCoy told about his job in a factory. He was driving a wheelbarrow at present, but in a week or two he would move up to using a broom.

"They got about more people hired keeping the place clean than they have making things. This is going to be my best job yet, I think," he said, "and

I'm not going to quit no matter who gets the best of me. If they lay me off they're going to have to tell me more than once to go. I got to thinking last night, and I can see you're all right about not going now. I'll drop you a line and let you know when I'm coming after you. I guess if you get too hard up for money before I get back, you could write one of the girls to send you a little. They got no families to keep." He sipped and set the cup down. "Tastes like your coffee and water had a law suit and the coffee come clear."

"Last grain of coffee in the house, and I been saving what I had for breakfast. Just can't hardly stand it without coffee," Mrs. McCoy said. "You'll have to go down to that store and get us a little bit of stuff. Twenty miles to town, and I got no transportation, and I don't want to ask Mr. Thompson for credit. Not been a dab of anything bought since you left, and we're scraping the bottom of the barrel. It's an awful long way for the younguns to carry stuff. And it'd be better if you'd get acquainted with him."

"It's the post office there too," Sara said.

Mr. McCoy patted Sara's head. "I barely got enough money to buy gas and oil back and pay my board, and I had to borrow some of it because I only got two days' pay. Maybe I can get some credit with the man."

They loaded into the car and bumped over the rocks and splashed through the creek to the store, which was closed. When they kept on honking, Mr. Thompson came out of the big green house under the hill, below the store.

"Closed on Sunday!" he shouted.

"Could open it up for a little trade. Today's the only time I have to haul in some stuff." Mr. McCoy got out and stretched, walked around the car and fastened a rattling radiator cap.

Mr. Thompson kept shaking his head till John Henry got out and called, "Mr. Thompson?" Then a smile lighted his face. "Oh, it's my herb and mail boy. And this is your pa, I reckon. Well, I guess I can open up in this case, but, mind you, I don't make it no habit for nobody."

He went back into the house for keys while they piled out of the car. When they were all inside the store, he closed the door. "I don't court Sunday trade. But a horse of another color's another color. You're Henry McCoy. The boy and girl's been down. This the missus and all?" Henry McCoy kept nodding his head in answer. "Guess you noticed the house you passed up the hollow there. Sure would like to sell it to a family'd take care of it. My own ma's old home place, it is. Been in the family, the land, since one of my grandpas bought more'n a thousand acres from the Indians for two shotguns and a round of powder. A mighty good trader, he was. All he done was trade. Look at it, you get time, and make me an offer."

"I couldn't even think of buying a house. Had a run of bad luck. But I'm going to get on my feet before long, sure am. What I want right now's a little credit to tidy my family over a few days. Pay you in a couple of weeks, at the latest."

Mr. McCoy looked a little sad, and John Henry felt sorry for him. He had heard his father say this before. Ever since he could remember, they had been going to get on their feet. If they had gone to Columbus, they would not have had to ask Mr. Thompson for credit. But they would have asked somebody else when they got there.

Mr. Thompson flushed angrily. "Credit's that horse of another color that's about rode me out of business. Got more on the books than I got in my pockets now." He looked down at the small faces

61

peering up at him, lined up like steps along the counter. When Clarabell said, "Hi," he grinned and said, "Hi yourself. Now, we could use some help around the place, and I can't see younguns go hungry. Our hard luck shouldn't make them go empty. Maybe you got something you can put up for a loan? Old gun or something?"

"Not a thing. All I got's my word."

Granny stood near the thread and needles, her eyes moving from box to box. Mrs. McCoy leaned on a sack of beans and waited. Sara walked to the door, acting bored with it all. Clarabell tugged at Mr. McCoy's knees until he lifted her to the counter, where she sat smiling and watching Mr. Thompson's hands tap up and down impatiently before he said, "No man's any better than his word. Never been beat by a McCoy yet on a store debt." He began filling a bag with items as Mr. McCoy read them from a paper. Clarabell kissed her father on the cheek and whispered in his ear.

Mr. McCoy twisted a curl at the top of her blond hair and said with the air of a man who will be generous, "Give these younguns about a quarter's worth of the biggest candy you got, the old woman

62

a couple a pounds of coffee. Ma, what're you pining for over there?"

Granny patted her apron pocket. "Something's happened to my thimble, and I can't hardly sew a dab. I believe there's one here to fit."

John Henry knew where her thimble was. But it was old and worn. Let her have a new one!

When Sara walked toward him, Mr. McCoy said, "You run your lip out any more, Sissie, and you'll step on it. What're you craving special?"

"Pop. I've not had any pop since a coon's age." Sara smiled now.

"A six-pack of pop. I believe you're the only one's not been heard from, John Henry."

"Nothing. I don't want a thing, thank you."

When the trading had ended, Mr. Thompson sniffed and rubbed his forehead. "How much rent you all a-paying? Could let you have my place, near a mile each way closer to everything, and a fine big house, a mite run down but warm and roomy, for ten dollars a month."

"Don't rightly know as I'm to pay anything. Man said move in. He was a-working where I was when I got laid off in Chicago, said it was his brother's

63

place a-setting empty, and I'd have to move if he ever wanted it, but they'd rather have somebody in it, afraid it might get accidentally burnt down by a hunter. Can't beat a deal like that. Never paid more'n five dollars for a house in a hollow in my life, but I sure do thank you for the offer." Mr. McCoy carried out a sack of flour and some lard. "Be back soon or send the money by mail."

"Don't rush off so," Mr. Thompson said. "Trade with you on that house."

The family had followed, each person with a bag or box of something. "Ready?" Mr. McCoy asked them. "Better roll. Have to head for Columbus."

"Could give you a job cutting some fence posts. Got a good timber job up there, if we can find a market for it," Mr. Thompson called.

"Sure thing," Mr. McCoy called, "if this job don't last." He drove away. "That man'd skin a gnat to get its tallow. Ten dollars? I wouldn't want to offer him five."

"Ought to get some apples," Granny said when they got to the old house. "Hard dragging for these little ole younguns, and they'll beat eating snowballs any cold day. Henry?" He passed the house without stopping. "Why didn't you stop, Henry?"

"In a hurry, Ma. You all get started poking around there, I'd never get started back. You-all don't care enough to go back with me." When Mrs. McCoy took a deep breath, he said, "Now, you know I was joking."

"Have to take what that man says with a grain of salt," Granny said.

"Car'd sure beat dragging them." Sara pushed John Henry a little, afraid he would make the Pepsi Cola warm by leaning on it.

He pushed back. "And who drags them?"

"Now, younguns, don't start fussing," Mrs. Mc-Coy said.

"Be two weeks before I get back, and you-all be good and ready. Get loose ends tied up. And, John Henry, you look after these womenfolks for me. They need a good strong man."

After lunch, Mrs. McCoy packed some clean clothes, a half dozen apples and a sandwich. They all hugged Mr. McCoy and watched the car until it was out of sight. Sara and Clarabell cried a little. John Henry sat down on the porch and examined the buckeyes and the turtle shell. He could hear the women as they stacked dishes and tidied the kitchen.

"Maybe we should have gone," Mrs. McCoy said.

Granny sighed. "Gone where? Now, Mary, you know good and well we can't go tagging off with not a roof to put over our heads. That's the reason he's so light footed, maybe, us getting so lonesome we just take off. No. You know we very nearly got put in jail, or something, one time, dragging around that bus station, waiting for him to find a place to go. I've got to live off the government, I might as well do it right here as anywhere. Now, Mary, I say after all these years of traveling from bad to worse we put a stop to it."

"Wish I'd gone," Sara said.

John Henry rocked the turtle shell back and forth with one finger, felt the spiny ridge inside it and laid the buckeye in it.

His mother said a little louder, "Henry's the boss, the way a man's supposed to be, and as his wife I do what he thinks is right. They just don't make a better man to his family. Lost the mold when they made him."

Granny's voice rose too. "Now hold your horses. I reckon I know Henry well as anybody. What he thinks is right might not always be. If the blind lead the blind, they all fall in the ditch. And you-all can do what you want to, but I been studying the last few days, and I've decided to stay somewhere, and this-here suits me, or near about it. Stay by myself. Nobody bothers anybody around here, and you know it. All I need's a good watchdog."

John Henry hurried with the turtle shell, set it on the window sill. "Might find us a good dog."

"Dog eat more than us all," Sara said. Granny glared at her, and she dropped her head so that her hair covered her face like a small tent.

John Henry could tell that his mother was taking her spite out on the shell. "What're you doing with that thing?"

"Keep it. Let you-all use it for a flower pot, if you like. You really want a dog, Granny? One was here. If somebody'll help me catch him, we might get him to stay."

Granny whispered to John Henry, "Let's me and you go down and get us a sack of apples. We keep on chasing rainbows, and the pot's never there."

Sara wanted to go along, but Mrs. McCoy put her to washing dishes. Clarabell went to add new rocks to the play well-box she was building.

John Henry and Granny did not speak until they reached the old house. They peeked through windows, rattled doors, walked around the fence and looked down a well with a stone box around it. They found apple, peach, pear, plum and cherry trees back of the house, and they found a smokehouse.

"Oh, I've always wanted one," Granny said. She leaned against the cold wall, and a smile of pleasure softened every line in her face. "Imagine anybody leaving a place like this. If it was mine, wild horses couldn't drag me off to no two-room loft where you can't spit without hitting somebody." The rotting smokehouse had a smell of rancid salt which she inhaled happily. "Don't guess we'd ever have any meat to smoke, but a smokehouse makes a fine place for keeping stuff you accumulate if you stay in one place long enough. My pa used hickory bark to smoke his meat. I ought to a been kicked, maybe, for ever selling my place, you know it?"

John Henry didn't know the place, except by hearsay, but Granny had talked about it so much that he could imagine it all—and it sounded like this place! Her old house had burned and the land was divided and had a highway through it now. It

69

would make her too sad to see it, she told Mr. Mc-
Coy once when he offered to drive her there.

"Sold it bit by bit, starting right after World
War I," she said.

John Henry had been busy watching a wood-
pecker circling a tree. He had come along to humor
her, but the more he looked at this place the better
he liked it. He couldn't remember ever having seen
a finer house. It was like a dream they couldn't
have. When Granny sneezed, he said, "We better
make tracks. This night air that'll be coming on soon
may give you a cold."

While they walked home, Granny talked of the
good life she remembered on the farm, of the good
places they had rented briefly, of the good neighbors
they had had a few times in the city. "People are
nice, you treat them nice, I find, and I'm going to
see if they all are, maybe come tomorrow." When
he asked what she meant, she said, "You'll see."

They peeled apples until the yard was pinpointed
with fireflies. "Nothing prettier under the sun, and
just listen to them frogs singing. Good to hear
something besides the roar of a truck or a train and
quarreling and the bang of somebody's television."

"Wish we had one," Sara said.

70

"Me too," Clarabell chimed in.

"Helps pass time in town, but we got things to do." Mrs. McCoy cocked her ear toward the hill. "Rain crow a-calling. Rains, we can't dry apples. Henry gets so lonesome for us he loses his judgment. Still, it makes me sad, letting him go off alone."

Sara finished the last apple she had to peel, got the pins and began rolling her long hair into flat circles. "Rains, how'll we get to school?"

"Same way we'd get there if it was dry, only we'd get there a little faster and be a little wetter, I reckon," John Henry answered.

Streaks of rain, driven by wind, lashed the windows the next morning. Mrs. McCoy refused to let them leave the house. At ten o'clock the sun came out.

"Too late now," Sara said sadly. "Let's look for a bee tree."

Granny chuckled. "Law, I want you to listen. Not enough tree blossoms nowdays for much wild honey, I guess. But it's something to think about. Might find us a swarm, come spring, and hive them up."

They spread some apples on an old coat. Within

71

a few minutes a dozen yellowjackets swarmed around the apples. Clarabell tried to chase them away, but she left them alone when she got stung on the end of the left little finger.

"Let's me and John Henry go and get some more apples," Granny said.

When they reached the house, Granny took a clean apron from her old apron pocket. She tied the clean one about her waist, hung the old one on the fence and kept on walking.

"You lost?" John Henry asked.

"Not much. It's not right for a woman to let her younguns boss her if they're small, so why should it be and them big? Come on, you want to see me trade some of that man's different color horses."

Granny didn't wait for Mr. Thompson to say anything before she began. "I've come on business, house business. I don't have ten cents to my name, but you've got a house going to waste. Needs a fire in it to dry out the rot. Needs somebody to love it. Houses are like people, they fall apart when nobody cares."

"What've you got?" Mr. Thompson combed his long gray hair with his fingers and worked his lips up and down like a rabbit.

"Nothing except the need for a house I love and some ground I can tend. Give you half on what I raise next year. Chase out the rats and bugs and cut down the trees shading things too much."

John Henry stood scratching the bottom of his right foot with the big toe of his left one. "I'll help Granny all I can," he said.

Mr. Thompson stood very still, looking down at John Henry. Then he smiled. "I do believe you will. My old woman had this-here land, and we built here so as to have a store, rented the house pretty good for a while. Then—" He snapped his fingers. "You help me and the old woman one day a month for the winter, and then half of what you raise next summer. A fair deal?"

Granny chuckled and clapped her hands. "Fair enough, sir. Don't tell nobody, but we're ready to start, and not a thing to work with. You loan us a hoe and a sharp knife and a broom, and we'll bring them back. And we want to charge some sulfur for some bleached apples. Loan us a barrel and we'll give you a mess when they're done."

John Henry rolled the barrel and Granny dragged the tools. When they got to the house, Granny said, "Sweep a mite and cut weeds."

John Henry looked up at the sun and decided it was past time for lunch. "Mommy'll be worried. We better go."

"Not much use a-carrying a load up. Let's take a few choice ones, come right straight back and get to work."

Mrs. McCoy had been worried, and she could not understand their wanting to go back and take Sara with them.

John Henry felt like a real pioneer, like Daniel Boone on the Wilderness Trail, as the horseweeds fell. "Timber," he shouted once, and Granny chuckled and stuck a chicken feather in the twist of white hair at the top of her head. He carried weeds and piled them at the back of the house while Sara and Granny cleared the smokehouse of shoes and rags covered with mold and bugs. John Henry gathered apples and washed the barrel while Granny and Sara nipped the ends of the apples to let the sulfur in. Soon the sulfur was burning in the barrel, and they lighted some garbage from the same match. While the garbage burned, they swept the porches and nailed down some loose boards.

"I'd like to know what you-all been up to," Mrs. McCoy said when they returned at dark.

"I'm a-going to try dyeing some rags for rugs with walnut hulls, like my ma used to do. When I was young, we made ink with pokeberries. Lots of nice poke stalks, be lots of greens come spring, can us up a batch then."

They sat for a while, and Granny remembered when they had made clothes from their own wool from their own sheep, had their own chickens and eggs, cows and horses, a little tad of cotton, a wee bit of tobacco, even a dab of broom corn. "Never run out to no stores every whipstitch. Wasn't no stores handy. Made our own soap and everything. That was living. I'd like to be living like that again, and I just may do it."

"Why'd you ever quit if you liked it so much?" Sara asked.

"Married off. Married your grandpa, bless him, a good man if ever there was one, but he had a bent to coal mining, and we sold off the land a dib at a time to pay bills between jobs and during mining strikes. I'd really like to farm again."

"I don't know what you-all've got up your sleeves. You can't plow concrete, and we'll be living in the city in a few weeks and you know it," Mrs. McCoy said. "Only dirt we own's that on these dirty feet around here that've got to be washed before we get into bed."

Clarabell pulled up her sleeve. "I've got a dirty elbow too," she said.

Five

John Henry woke early. He wanted to get started to school and to get started learning, but he lay very still thinking for a while.

What if Miss Day let him know she was disappointed in his missing so much school? What if the children began teasing him about being stuck-up for having lived in town? He couldn't blame Miss Day, for certain. He would keep his mouth shut;

he'd learned that much. He would say a flat *I*, if he said it, not roll it around and make two syllables, the way people said it in Cleveland.

School had been a little frightening at times, a giant that swallowed him in its many rooms, and he got lost and cried. Hundreds and hundreds of students and teachers. Miss Short, who was tall, taught second grade in Chicago, and said, "I'm going to send you to the principal." That was the second week, and the kids had told him the principal kept an electric paddle. John Henry didn't see the paddle, but he couldn't see very much with his eyes closed and he couldn't say much with his mouth shut. He stood there in the office, like a tree stump—no, more like a turtle—and he couldn't tell anyone why he cried so much.

He had been given a test in the first grade in Cleveland, and he hadn't known what a lot of silly-looking things were. Miss Brown had shown the test paper to the principal when he came to visit. John Henry heard them talking about the test measuring something he hadn't known he had, something they called an IQ. Miss Brown called one of the things pictured on the paper a top, but he couldn't name something he hadn't seen, could he? The whirligigs he'd seen had been called dancers, and his father could make two of them by whittling a thread spool in two and putting sharpened sticks in the ends. He knew whistles they didn't know about, whittled from a willow branch, grass blades held between the thumbs, and he could nearly split their ear drums by blowing between his fingers. How was he to know their dancers were big as balloons and had stripes or that their whistles had chains on them? But Miss Brown did brag on him one day for keeping the paper picked up around his seat.

He had a cold and missed so many days in Chicago they got a man to come to the house and threaten his father with something he called a fine, but which sounded terrible. And he got put in the "slow" class. The slow class made things from clay, which was so much fun he pulled off his shoes one day and made footprints in the little pone of clay; he squeezed until the brown clay came up between his toes, like real clay on a creek bank did. The teacher hadn't seen any fun in it, not when she found the clay had stained the new tile on the floor!

School hadn't all been sad, but it was sad when Miss Merry, on Blackberry Mountain, found he could "say" a whole page of a book but didn't really know a word on it. He had been in first grade for months and months and had memorized the pages by listening to the other students recite. She showed him that all the chicken-track squiggles on the page were not alike. The telephone poles were *I* or small *L* and doughnuts were *O*'s. *N* was a mountain and *M* was two mountains. After a while he knew the letters and was reading silly stuff like, "Here I come. Look, look, see me go. See me go, go, go." And he continued to play-like he was one of the children in the pictures and lived in a fine white house and had expensive toys.

When he entered a big school, somebody always said, "I don't think you belong in here." How could he belong when he couldn't even find his room if he went outside? After he learned to read numbers it was a little better. One time he was put back a grade, and he was the oldest pupil in the class, and the biggest one. John Henry liked it most when he was the best reader in class. Last year he was the best reader in his group for three whole months at Pigeon Roost School, and that was when he began really wishing that he could stay put. No, he had wished it for months and months, maybe years and years, but it was at Pigeon Roost that he began wishing it over and over every day. They moved on Thanksgiving Day, and he begged the family not to go. His father took him behind the house, as the last of Granny's quilts were being loaded, and explained about jobs and education and the man of the house having to take care of the family the best way that he could, and John Henry had, while they were talking man-to-man, promised to be the man of the house whenever his father had to be away.

Granny whispered, "John Henry? We got a lot of work to do."

Now he wished he hadn't carried the apples, hadn't let Granny get so excited about the house. "I thought I was going to school," he said.

"Now you wouldn't let Granny down, would you? I got to thinking I'd have to have you to help, and this move'll keep you in school."

He felt sad about letting her down, but he thought he'd better go to school before the teacher got tired of his wasting time and getting further and further behind. For once, he would love to hear a teacher say, "I do believe you're getting ahead, John Henry." Then Granny was whispering again.

"Them apples'll beat a snowball this winter too."

John Henry liked eating snowballs, but they

81

didn't do much toward filling the stomach. Still, he would let his stomach go empty if he could get ahead in school and stay put all year. But a week or two was maybe better than no school, and he would not tell Miss Day he was leaving. When he did that, teachers shrugged and stopped worrying very much about his not paying attention in class or not learning new reading words or arithmetic steps. Where the good feeling had been there was suddenly an empty place, a sunk-in place.

"Won't be so far to school," Granny said, "and no creek crossing."

He didn't mind the far, and he didn't mind the creek, not now anyway.

Granny continued, "Won't take off, stay right there like a groundhog in its hole. Plant a garden come spring, and well—John Henry, we'll put down roots."

John Henry snorted in his disappointment. "We've been going to do that time and again. Next move."

"Trust me. There's an end to the line, any line, and this is it. Be only another day or two you'll miss."

Sara stirred. "What is it?"

"Shh, let's get up and get started. Haul your-self out quiet now, surprise your mommy with how industrious we are," Granny whispered back.

"Let me handle this," Granny said when they were at the table.

Mrs. McCoy sipped coffee appreciatively before speaking. "This is the first time you've all stirred before breakfast in a long time. What kind of tonic are you on?"

Granny kept her eyes on the piece of bread she was crumbling over the gravy and potatoes. "Mountain air and things to do. We're fixing up the Thompson place down the hollow."

Mrs. McCoy's mouth dropped open. "Why would anybody in their right mind waste time on that old house?"

"To live in. Not as crazy as you think, when you look at it."

Mrs. McCoy held the cup in midair. "Henry's job's up there. We'll be up there right away, and you know it."

"He might could get a job here sooner or later. If he can, he can, and if he can't, he can't. We're done with being on the road like bums, shifting from pillar to post. Closer to the store and post office and school. Good well and everything." If Granny had been talking about a palace, she wouldn't have sounded happier.

Mrs. McCoy shook her head. "We've never stuck out long by ourselves."

John Henry could see his mother was interested. She could always see and hear both sides of a problem and agree a little with both sides.

"This is for staying put," Granny said as she spooned fried apples onto Clarabell's plate. "We'll have to hear what Henry has to say later. And you don't have to lift a hand to help, Mary. We're doing fine."

Mrs. McCoy thought for a minute. "You'd keep the younguns out of school to mess around down there? They need to be in school. It's hard to make up lost time in school."

"Won't be the first time they've missed, but it might be the last time for a while. First few days they don't do much anyway." Granny rose from the table. "Time's a-wasting."

The work was more than Granny had thought. By ten o'clock John Henry had made two piles of junk from the house and collected two bird nests, and Granny and Sara had swept the walls and floors of the first floor. When Mr. Thompson came at twelve, John Henry was tacking some heavy paper over a broken window.

"We got a room apiece," Sara said. "First time we had six rooms. Besides upstairs."

"Thought I'd tell you that well needs cleaning," Mr. Thompson said as he took the hammer and tacked a small nail into a window frame.

"Clean as we've been used to having," Granny said.

"House's been leaking, and I can't roof it," he said.

"Pans'll catch water till we get it patched."

"May be ghosts."

Granny looked up from sprinkling sand on the floor. "Never saw a ghost I couldn't get the best of. You a-trying to back us out?"

"Hate to see you move in and right back out. Last family left in two days. March, it was, and they'd plowed the garden. One family before that stayed a week."

"Pooh," Granny snorted. "John Henry, you cover that hoe with some rags, and Sara you get started scrubbing in here."

Mr. Thompson followed Granny to the next room. "You stay the winter out and patch up around, won't need to work that day we bargained for. How's that?" Granny went to the smokehouse to check on the sulfur burning in the barrel, and Mr. Thompson followed. John Henry pulled water from the well slowly so he could hear. "And anything you find's yours to use however you see fit. That's our rule on anything that's been left."

"Fine, real fine, Mr. Thompson. I'm going to need some stuff. Charge it to me, and I'll work it off later washing or sewing or something. Nails, window glass, roofing."

By evening they were tired. They were far from having the place fixed up, but Granny was ready for moving the next morning.

"I never said I was moving," Mrs. McCoy told her.

"Pout and suit yourself," Granny said. "I'll batch down there. You're old enough to make up your own mind, and I'm not going to beg you. That bed I sleep in's mine, and I've got quilts and things. Got a good fireplace for cooking. Enough old pots and buckets thrown around down there to make out."

"I couldn't let you go by yourself," Mrs. McCoy said.

The few things grew heavy before they got everything carried to the house. When night came, they were too tired to do anything except eat the beans that had been cooking all day on the fire. They unrolled mattresses on the floor and lay down on them.

John Henry was first to hear the thump and whine and the long, low "wooo." After a while Granny stirred.

"Ghost?" John Henry asked.

"No."

"What is it?"

"How would I know? Just something."

Mrs. McCoy lit the lamp. There was nothing in any of the rooms. The clock had not been wound, and it was not running. Clarabell began to cry.

"If I didn't know this was September, I'd swear it was Halloween," Sara said.

After a while they decided to set up the beds and put things where they belonged. Shortly before daylight they lay down for naps, and the day was half gone before John Henry woke.

Sitting on the edge of the bed, he looked out the window. The sun was shining and a patch of goldenrod was waving in the wind. He was angry with himself, and he stamped his foot on the floor.

Mrs. McCoy was smearing flour paste under bits of wallpaper at the end of his bed. "What's the matter?" she asked. "Mad because I didn't wake you? I couldn't, good as you were sleeping. Lots of things to learn at home, and one's not to lose your temper, and another's to use the manners you worked so hard to learn."

"Yes mam, and I'm sorry, Mommy." To show that he was sorry, he picked some goldenrod and arranged it in a brown apple-butter jar.

Then he went to help Granny make a kiln for the apples from a piece of tin. He walked out a little farther, back of the house, and found a small pumpkin, a few hills of potatoes and a row of onions.

He helped Sara squeeze some pokeberries and put the red juice into a jar. He made a feather pen. The pen didn't write very well, but the juice made good paint, and they played Indian for a while.

"When're we going to get the stove? I'm tired of that old bread fried at the fireplace," Sara told Granny.

"I'll show you the real pioneer way," Granny said.

She stirred down some hot coals, set an iron skillet of cornbread mix on them and covered the pan tightly. She set five potatoes and five onions to roasting in the coals beside the pan.

"All that's missing is a cow. For two cents, I'd

see if we couldn't borrow us one," Granny said. "When I was a girl, lots of people had cows to loan. All they wanted was that you give them back the calves. They wanted you to raise a calf for them every year."

"What about the boogerman?" Clarabell asked.

"We were all tired last night and we remembered what Mr. Thompson said. Now, let's go outside for a breath of fresh air," Mrs. McCoy answered.

When they were on the porch, Granny said, "You remember the old sunbonnets women used to wear, Mary? I've left my last one somewhere, but I'm going to cut me a pattern and make me one. Sun turns me brown as a bear." She took Clarabell on her lap. "Make the baby a bonnet too."

Mrs. McCoy remembered some songs they hadn't sung for a while. She and Granny took turns lining off the verses of "Pretty Polly" and "Darling Corie" and "Barbara Allen."

"How about my song?" John Henry asked after a while.

Granny's voice rose high and clear.

"John Henry was a little bitty baby. He sat on his mammy's knee.

He picked up a hammer, and a little piece
of steel,
Said, 'This hammer'll be the death of me.
Lawd, Lawd, this hammer'll be the death
of me.' "

Granny cleared her throat, "Been some that say
that song was about some of your kinfolks, way
back, John Henry. Your grandpa was called John
and your daddy's called Henry. They say, was your
great grandpa became a miner and changed the song
for himself. Your grandpa used to sing it to me.
Let's see if I can remember how it goes." She
paused, then sang:

"John Henry was a big, big baby.
He stood by his papa's knee.
He picked up a shovel, a pick, and a light,
Said, 'Coal mining'll be the death of me.' "

Then Granny asked, "You going to be a coal
miner?" John Henry thought for so long she said,
"Cat got your tongue?"
"Thinking. I don't know. I don't like a big dark
hole in the ground. Be like a mole, but I might.
Might have my own mine someday. No running

around and moving. I'd plain stay put all the time."

Sara hummed for a minute before she began singing.

> "John Henry was a stay put boy.
> He leaned on his granny's knee.
> He picked up a—

What'd he pick up?" she asked.

"How about a pumpkin?" Mrs. McCoy answered. "That's about the biggest thing on a farm—unless it was a calf or a colt."

"Better hit the hay," Granny said.

A pounding noise woke John Henry in the night. Granny was taking boards from the door at the top of the stairs. Mrs. McCoy was shouting above the sound, "You can't see a thing once you get it open. Do wish you'd let it alone. Feel safer with that door nailed shut. Not staying here another night. I've got to have some rest."

John Henry was out of bed before his mother could finish saying, "Get back in there." He pressed down on the hammer handle, and the board came off with a bang. The door swung open on the blackest black he'd ever seen, and there was a strange whirring sound, like a fan.

"You hold the light, and I'll look around," Granny ordered.

He eased forward. In the shadows, beyond the small circle of light, he could see old furniture, boxes and barrels. Granny peered into the nearest barrel. Dishes. She bent over a box. Clothes. Then John Henry looked up at the ceiling. Bats! There were bats everywhere!

He was shivering so the words were far apart. "It's bats. Hurry, shut the door!" He backed from the room. "Mommy, your boogerman's bats."

"None of this mess's mine," Mrs. McCoy said. But then she added, "How'll we get them out? They could bite."

It was settled almost at once that they would get the bats out and close whatever openings they might have. Tomorrow.

Then John Henry remembered something. "You think the bats made that whistling sound?"

Granny tucked cover around the sleeping Sara before answering, "I don't, but we'll find it. Hard to tell what-all we'll find up there."

John Henry did not speak of school the next

morning. They had to get rid of the bats and find the noise. Granny and John Henry opened the windows, lighted some rags and left them to smoke in a dishpan while they went out to salvage whatever was in the two boxes they carried down with them. After a while they returned to shovel out the bats that had not flown away.

They carried things outside then—a broken bedstead, several chairs, two small tables, a large mirror, some lamps, a mattress. Sara found books in one of the boxes, magazines in another. There were butter churns crammed with mouse traps and fly swatters, an ox yoke someone had started to paint red. And everything smelled of mold and smoke. When it was all spread on the porches and in the yard for airing, they returned to clean the room. Granny swept the morning-glory-patterned walls and ceilings. John Henry was brushing away spider webs when the broom struck something lumpy underneath the paper. An empty bottle had been poked into a crack under a window, with its flat bottom turned into the room and its open neck outside. He tugged until it was loose.

"I think that's the noise," John Henry said. He blew into the bottle, and it was the same sound, only not quite the same.

"Wind striking the bottle just right could do it," Mrs. McCoy said, laughing a little at the scare they'd all had. "But why in the world was it ever stuck there?"

Granny sneezed and sniffed. "I'm trying to think why, but I can't at this minute. I'm going to have to get outside awhile. All this dust is stopping up my head."

Sara had been standing watching sometimes, sometimes looking at a magazine of paper-doll cutouts she had found. "I'm going to have me a room up here," she said.

"You're counting chickens before the eggs hatch." Mrs. McCoy pushed the broom against the floor, trying to straighten the end that had become warped with the sweeping. "If I know you, little girl, when your daddy comes back you'll forget about this room and be ready to go to Columbus so fast it'll make your head swim." She looked about, appreciating the space. "If we do stay, we'll have room for all the married younguns to come and visit. Had us some more bedding, we could have a right nice summer bedroom here."

Granny had been standing by the door, waiting to hear and to see everything. "Counting eggs before they hatch is better than not counting at all, Mary.

95

And we just might talk Henry into settling here. Could be a job open up by spring."

To show that Granny wasn't the boss, Mrs. Mc-Coy said, "I think he's big enough to make up his own mind." Then to demonstrate that she wasn't offended and hadn't meant an offense, she took Granny by the elbow and led her down the stairs. "Why don't we go find us a setting-down chore and let these younguns finish tidying up here?"

"I'm tired," Sara complained, still holding the magazine.

"You go set too," John Henry said. "And I'll stay up here awhile."

Six

Granny looked out the window on Friday morning and said, "Rain before seven, quit before eleven. And bad as you're itching to get back to school, I don't think you'd better mess up the week now, much as we got to do." When John Henry dropped his head, she said, "Spring, we could use John Henry's nose to plow. But it's fall, so lift it up and let's get that old stove down and a bit more patching done."

When the moving and patching had been done, Granny tried her hand at dyeing some rug material with spongy greenish-brown walnut shells. The rags were not as pretty as John Henry had expected them to be, but Granny was pleased and stood back to admire them when they were spread on the old rail fence. On Saturday he carried wood and coal enough to do through a rainy week while Sara cut rags and wound them into balls and Granny finished his new shirt.

When Monday came, he wore the new shirt, carried the book under his arm and a giant-size brownish-red apple in his hand, along with a small grubby bag with two smaller apples for his lunch. Along the road, houses perched like crows, a little black from soot and gray from age. Here and there he saw a white house, a pink one, a green one and a blue one. He could hear shouts of children at play when he turned the last curve in the road. Then there was the school, not quite as white as he had remembered it, not as big, a little higher off the ground, and the yellow clay yard some smaller.

Miss Day was standing on the porch with a small bell in her hand, and for a minute she was not as pretty as he had remembered.

She smiled and said, "New students?" John Henry gave her the apple and the book. Her smile grew larger. "Oh, I remember you now. What a nice apple."

He had hoped she would bite into the apple immediately. She rang the bell, waited until the line of boys and the line of girls got very straight and quiet, nodded for them to enter and be seated. Then she walked up the center of the room and laid the apple on her desk. The apple kept being pushed a little, with books and papers—pushed a little more. Soon it was at the edge of the desk, was going to fall and split open.

John Henry raised his hand. When she nodded at him, he walked to the desk and said, "Your apple's going to fall."

She looked up from a paper where she was marking a word, and he expected her to say, "You want it? Somebody gave it to me." Instead, she said, "You know, I forgot about the apple you gave me. I'll have it to enjoy at lunch. Thanks again, John Henry."

Reading class began. Students hopped up like rabbits from their holes, read and popped back. When it came his turn, John Henry did not know where to read and Miss Day passed him with a smile, "For today. You must keep up."

Then there was English. Miss Day said, "Sometimes we hear people use the wrong word for burst. Who can give the right forms for burst and rise?"

Somebody said, "Rise, rose, riz." There was laughter. The red-haired girl sitting in front of John Henry said, "When it's time for breakfast, Mommy lets me bust the biscuits."

"She lets you open the canned biscuits? That's nice." Miss Day stood up. "I guess everybody's here by now." She counted. "Forty-four. We have one hundred per cent attendance today. Now, will you please raise your hand when I call your name." She started reading from a green-backed book. "Abbie Addams, June Addams, Lizzie Baker, Silas Brown . . ." When she called his name, John Henry threw his hand up so quickly it struck a braid lying on his desk and threw it into the air.

"He's bothering me, teacher, this new boy, he pulled my hair," the girl said, and she stood, making a stupid face at him to show her disapproval.

"Nancy, please," Miss Day said.

"He pulled my hair, and if he fools with me I'll snatch him bald-headed!"

100

"I never pulled. I touched her accidentally, and I'm sorry," John Henry said.

Miss Day nodded. "John Henry, you and Sara have missed a whole week of school. Could you tell me why? You're getting off to a bad start."

"It rained some, and we moved away." He kept his eyes on Nancy's braid, which still dragged across his desk, and he moved the desk a little.

"Moved away? You're still here."

"Yes mam, I get so used to moving away. This time, though, we just moved a ways down the hollow, some closer." He stood. There was a puzzled look on the teacher's face. "You see we had to wade the creek eight times, four up and four down, and we found another house on down closer."

"And that took all week?" Miss Day looked at Sara.

John Henry sat down, and Sara stood. "No mam, not that took all week. The house, we thought, had ghostes in it, at least Mommy did."

Nancy giggled, and Miss Day said, "Shh. The word is ghosts, not ghostes."

"No mam, it was bottles and bats," Sara said.

"Have you noticed how nicely John Henry and Sara talk?" Miss Day asked of the entire room.

101

"It's because we've lived all over. We've lived in Chicago and Cincinnati and Detroit and—everywhere."

John Henry tried to catch Sara's eyes and tell her to stop, but she kept on twisting a curl on the side of her cheek, pulling the wispy hair until it was like a muddy icicle.

"You and John Henry stay in at recess, and I'll try to find some books for you. Did you bring your report cards?"

A boy straight across from John Henry grinned as John Henry shook his head. It was the one who shoved him that first day. "Too bad. We play ball at recess, but I bet you couldn't hit the side of a barn anyway."

"Silas Brown, no whispering," Miss Day said.

John Henry didn't mind staying in. He never minded if it gave him a chance to talk with the teacher. Maybe she would ask him what he wanted to learn.

But she was very busy asking, "What can you read? What have you read?" She didn't have the kind of books they had read last year, and they didn't know the kind they could read by looking at the covers, so Miss Day asked a big girl to let

103

them try out. John Henry did fairly well in fourth grade, and Sara could pass for third.

"I'll let you stay in fourth, if you can keep up. Think you can?" Miss Day asked John Henry.

"Yes mam," he said. If there was one thing on earth he wanted to do now it was to keep up. "But I never did learn to borrow." He hated to say it, but she was getting ready for arithmetic, and he might as well get this part of it over with.

"We're adding today. You can carry, can't you?"

John Henry and Sara were fine in arithmetic that day. Then fourth through eighth grade was supposed to have science together, although each grade had different books. The subject was trees, and John Henry's book had nothing about trees. He turned through it quickly. How to let bread mold. "I bet I've seen more moldy bread than nearly anybody," he thought. He turned a page. Planting seeds in a glass and watching them sprout. "And the right place for seeds is the good warm ground." Watching steam from a kettle. "Pooh." Maybe someday he'd write a science book.

Three eighth-grade girls read about roots and trunks and leaves, about trees needing soil and water and sunlight. John Henry leaned forward.

Nancy had her finger at a page that was black with little white balls and long circle lines. Earth. Moon. John Henry had watched the astronauts land on the moon. Granny said she didn't believe it, said it was all made up, and the government would do better to use the money here on earth for some roads and for growing food for people who never had enough in some other countries.

Miss Day asked, "Any questions?" John Henry whispered to Silas Brown, because he wanted Silas to know he wasn't mad about the shoving or the remark about the ball game. "Why don't we talk about the astronauts?"

Silas repeated the question out loud, and Miss Day shook her head. "We don't any of us know enough about it, and we have to stick to our schedule." After a minute she seemed to be explaining just for John Henry. "I'm trying to get used to it all myself. Spelling, reading, arithmetic for eight grades, but a few things like science and social studies we have to combine the best we can and listen in when books don't match. With only fifteen minutes for each class, if we get off the subject some other class will be missed."

John Henry wasn't sure he understood about

schedules, but he thought she must be mighty smart. He nodded in answer, and Miss Day smiled.

He waited at lunch and at evening recess for someone to invite him outside to join the ball game. When no one did, he read about planets in the science book.

Then it was time to go home. John Henry tried to think of something to tell Granny. She always wanted to know what they'd learned. Sara hoped Granny would forget to ask, for they couldn't name anything. Sara decided to beat her to it. She asked before they reached the steps where Granny was sewing: "What've you been doing all day?"

Granny told about pasting back loose paper on the kitchen walls, making one dandy chair from two they had found upstairs and trimming down one leg on an old table so that it now stood perfectly straight in the front room. "We just may buy some of this stuff from Mr. Thompson sometime," Granny said. "Get some wire to patch up that set of old bedsprings, and we can fix us up another bed."

When Granny had finished, John Henry said quickly, "And what've you been doing, Mommy?" She had cleaned two old pickling churns, just in case they ever needed them, and had found an egg

106

basket filled with Christmas decorations and a roll of turkey-platter paper, which she might paste on the dining room wall. And she had washed a load of old coats and shirts.

"You didn't, by any chance, stop at the post office, did you?" Mrs. McCoy asked. "Your daddy may write any day."

After supper, they helped Granny rake leaves and pull weeds from the front yard. "If we had clover on this, we could raise us some bees for honey," Granny said.

Sara found a penny. Clarabell found a four-leaf clover. Granny found three nails and a piece of chain. John Henry found a horseshoe.

"Let's nail it above the front door," Granny said. "Horseshoe's supposed to bring good luck. High time we had some."

"Our teacher in Columbus one time laughed about that kind of thing," Sara said while drawing lines for hopscotch. "Super—super something or other she called it. Laughed about fortune-telling and planting by the moon."

"A little book learning goes to some people's heads," Granny said when the horseshoe was up. "I've seen more plantings than she'll ever see, and

107

I know taters grow big and come to the top of the ground, right out of the dirt, if they're planted in the light of the moon, and they go on down in the dark of the moon. Light-moon taters are big as your double fist, green peelings."

"Next year we could try some both times and see. Do a real experiment," John Henry said.

"And beans, planted the wrong time, bloom their heads off and no beans. Lye soap on the light of the moon'll foam up thick and stay soft as butter."

Mrs. McCoy shivered. "Evening's started cooling. Be frost and ice splinters before you know it. If I stayed here long, I'd have the house wired. Lights and a good iron. Granny, I got a feeling you ought to get out the cards and read what's ahead."

Granny got the worn cards that were kept in her sewing basket and were not for play. Long ago Clarabell had chewed up the lucky card, the seven of hearts, and it had been replaced by a six which wasn't needed in the reading. Granny shuffled the cards, gave them to John Henry for cutting. She shuffled them again, laid out two "surprise" cards, then dealt the rest, saying aloud, "Past, present, future," as she tossed the cards, face up, in three piles. She did not read the past, because she already knew the past. The present was full of kings and queens and jacks, which she did not know about, except that they meant people. "Looks like a lot of folks are having a hand in our lives right now." The future. "Oh, there's the lucky card in the future, John Henry. Did you wish something good?"

He had forgotten to wish while cutting the cards! He could have wished—oh, he could have wished anything! Then would the lucky-wish card have made it come true? Or would the card have, somehow, fallen into another pile? He had been wishing all day, every day for so many things. Maybe one of the back-wishes would count. He crossed his fingers, pecked on the porch post, looked back at the horseshoe above the door and wished for a friend, a real, true, honest friend.

"He wished for—oh, let's see now—he wished for money," Sara said and ducked from the playful slap he aimed at her.

"A pony, wish us a pony," Clarabell said. Granny had been telling of a pony she had when she was a girl and how her father sold it because she didn't want to ride a sidesaddle, the proper way for young ladies to ride. "I'll ride a sidesaddle, Granny, if you'll get me a pony."

Granny nodded, then shook her head. "We don't

109

ever seem to live at the getting place any more. Looks like a journey in store for somebody. Might be for the king of clubs there."

"I don't want a journey," John Henry thought. "I've had enough. I don't want . . . I want . . ." Granny continued reading the future cards, but his ears closed to the sounds around him, and he sat there thinking, "I want to stay . . ."

Sara poked him. "Time to go in. What's wrong with you anyway?"

There was a sound almost as quiet as fog rising or the sun going down. It could be Fido walking on the dew-damp leaves and grass.

Mrs. McCoy tapped his shoulder. "Time all honest farmers were in bed."

"Mommy, let me stay a little spell longer. Maybe I need some night air."

Granny patted his head, right in the top where she had gapped his hair the last time she cut it. "You're not coming down with something?"

He shook his head, and her fingers felt good in his hair. "You all go on in, and I'll lock up. Please?"

His mother stood in the door, under the horseshoe. "I never did go to bed and leave you up, but I guess you're growing up. Want anything?"

"No mam, and thank you," he said.

He wanted to shout at her and Granny, shout so loudly his daddy would hear all the way to wherever he was. He wanted to wish back to the time before Granny had said the word "journey." So far, Miss Day hadn't been as nice as she might have. But she'd been nicer than he figured he could be, given a roomful of grades one through eight and no doodads or aids or frills—just a stove, a water bucket, a paddle and a few worn-out books. He rubbed the buckeye for luck. None of the students had been especially nice either, but he was still new to them, and they were new to him, and it took time for the newness to wear off. He was still a stranger, and he didn't want to be a stranger all his born days. After a while, it could be my teacher and my school and my books and my lessons, and maybe, maybe if he got lucky, my friends.

He opened his eyes wide and turned them up to the sky to dry out. And there was a star, one big bright star. Wishing on a star might be the same as a card-cutting wish. It had to be a good wish, not just one for himself, and he had to hurry. If he blinked before saying it, or if he saw another star—

He whispered, "I want us to settle down and—"

111

Before he could finish the wish, something touched his hand. Something cool and wet. Something alive. A rough tongue spread out over his fingers. "Fido, Fido, you're back," he said, and it was as though his wish were already true.

He patted his foot and hummed a little. The tune was "Pretty Polly," but the words were his own.

"Oh Fido, oh Fido, right here you stand, with dew on your whiskers and—and burrs in your coat." It didn't rhyme, but poems didn't always have to rhyme, so why did songs?

With his arm around the dog, he hummed another one that he made up as he went along. "When John Henry was a middle-sized boy, he sat—he sat in the far-country. He patted a dog and he patted his foot, said, 'This is the life for me.'"

Seven

The early Tuesday morning sky was red and Granny predicted rain. It rained at recess, and John Henry went to stand on the end of the porch, to get away from the noise of so many conversations inside.

Silas Brown came to face him. "What do you do at recess in town?"

John Henry would have welcomed a friendly question. The tone of this one was not friendly, and

113

Silas did not look friendly. His neck and shoulders were too stiff, and he kept working his lips over his teeth and flexing his fingers. John Henry shook his head and leaned a little closer to the wall, moved back a step or two from the edge of the porch.

"You think you're too good to talk to me? Think living in town's made you a fine hair and smarter and better?" When there was no answer, Silas stepped closer, crowding him against the wall.

"Si Brown, you behave now or I'll tell on you for picking on people." It was the red-haired girl, Nancy, playing Slap Hands with Sara and forgetting that she had been picking on him herself not long ago.

"Keep your jib out of my business," Si growled at her before continuing with John Henry. "I'd as soon fight as anything. I bet you're a softie, and run scared." John Henry's tongue was frozen, and he shook his head. "You better run tomorrow, 'cause I'm going to whip you fair and square if you show up here."

John Henry's voice came out at last, a small squeak. "Why?"

"Because I'm champion, see. Best fighter in the whole school. Whip every strange boy comes here.

And I'm going to make you say Amen. If you want to say it, maybe I won't have to whip you. Say it right now. Say, 'Si Brown's the best fighter at Licking Branch School.' "

John Henry shook his head.

"And I'm richer'n anybody. That's why they don't like me, but I don't care. You better say it."

He edged toward John Henry, but John Henry stood very still. The girls were catching water that dripped from the house and slinging it on the half dozen boys who had now wandered out to the porch. A drop of water hit John Henry in the eye, but he did not blink until he said, "How do I know it?"

"You better believe me. I've made it so hot on a lot of boys they quit school, big boys too. How're you feeling?"

He thought quickly. "Cold. Plum cold right this minute." He had never liked fighting for real. Play fighting, he did like. He wished the boy would not push him against the wall. If he had to quit school— it was too much to even think about! He thought of telling Miss Day, but Miss Day couldn't really stop the fight. She could only punish them when it was over.

John Henry worried about the trouble with Si that night after he went to bed. He thought of staying home the next morning, but that would only postpone it all. When Sara wanted to wait for him, he said a little gruffly, "Go ahead, and you stay out of my business, no matter what that business may be." She ran ahead then, a little hurt. Even if Si didn't want to fight clean, John Henry didn't want Si to claim later that he was a sissy and had been helped by a girl. He would explain to Sara on the way home. What if the other boys joined Si? It was a chance he had to take. None of them had acted as if they cared a hoot for Si. None of them had offered to protect him either.

Si was waiting for him. He stood a few feet off the school grounds, on the rocky creek bank. "You want to say Amen?" he asked.

"Why should I dirty my hands with you?" John Henry asked, sounding much braver than he felt.

"Because you won't take my word that I'm champion. Because I got to prove that city slickers are yellow."

"Fight! You started it, Si," a big boy shouted.

"Ready?" Si sniffed and wiggled his shoulders. "Say it."

116

"Put your fist where your mouth is," another boy called.

"Move over here." John Henry pointed to a grassy spot, away from the rocks. He moved and took off his shirt as he went. He sunk his bare toes into the grass and rocked back and forth. He already knew that living in a city wasn't much, not the way they'd had to live, crowded and shifting about like worms in a can, and with nowhere to go and nothing to see except the concrete streets and sidewalks that were littered with garbage, but he couldn't say so now.

"You going to fight, or you going to keep hunting you a soft spot to get knocked out on?" Si had his shirt off now and was rubbing his right fist as if he were polishing it. "Case you didn't know it, that's my grandad's house you took over."

A crowd was gathering, pushing in. John Henry wanted to run. He wanted to beg Si to go away. But he would never be allowed to go to Licking Branch School if he did either of these. He would have to watch every move, but there was a chance. The best advantage he could have was to make Si Brown believe he was sure of himself. "I don't want to dirty my hands on you." He measured Si with his

117

eyes, and Si wasn't as big as he'd remembered him. Si looked as if he'd like to back out now. "You can't swallow my head, even if you bite it off." He saw from the puzzled look that Si didn't understand. He made fists, not very tight so they would look bigger. "Why should I use up my good fists on you when I plan to win the Golden Gloves, maybe?"

Si polished the other fist. "What? Talk some sense, if you can."

The crowd pushed closer, wanting some action. "Like two banty roosters. Going to strut around and threaten. Is that all?" "Hit him, John Henry." "Fight like the little boy you are, Si." "Put up or hush up," they called.

"A clean fight?" John Henry asked. "Turnabout's fair play, and if you don't fight clean—" His voice cut off on a high note. He couldn't think how the sentence should end, and he hoped it sounded like a threat.

"He's got Si buffaloed," someone said. Another person shouted, "You call people yellow, Si? You're so yellow you're orange."

Si came at him, and John Henry stepped to the side. He threw a punch that opened out as it reached Si. He grabbed Si's hand and pumped it up

118

and down while Si tried to get a handful of hair.

"You call this fighting?" Si shouted.

Si broke the hold and came at him again. John Henry slid. Si charged and fell on him. He grabbed Si's hands and rolled on the dew-wet grass. In a minute, John Henry was on top. He sat there, holding Si's hands, weighting down the squirming legs and riding Si as if he were a horse, thumping up and down. Then he slid off, took Si by the feet and turned him so that Si was beating the ground with his fists. When the bell rang, John Henry was still holding Si.

"Give up, Si." "Turn him loose, John Henry." "Boo." "Lion got bearded in his own den." "Boo." "Teacher'll straighten you all up, wait and see."

Si said, "Oh, shoot. You let me up, and I'll show you how to fight."

"You're licked, and you might as well say it," Nancy said.

John Henry gave him a little shake, and Si rolled his head and licked his lips. "Turn me loose," he said.

"Not till you say you're whipped. I'll hold you till it thunders," John Henry threatened bravely, but he was tired. If Si didn't give up in a minute, he might lose the hold. "Give up?"

120

Si worked his lips, wet them, then panted, "Give up."

John Henry released him quickly and stepped back, ready to defend himself if Si had been faking.

"Say, you're pretty good. Give me a hand here." Si held out his hand.

"Why'd you treat me like this, Si Brown?" John Henry still stood back, not trusting Si completely.

The crowd left, ran to line up at the door. Si continued to sit there with his hand out. "Oh, I been sizing you up. City slickers, soft, proud talkers, high shouldered, nose cutting, I can't stand. But you're not one." He grabbed at John Henry's hand, and John Henry backed a step, afraid this was a trick. "Throw me my shirt," Si said. John Henry put on his shirt and gave Si his hand.

They walked together. "Where'd you learn to fight like that?" Si asked.

"Use to be hours and hours of wrestling on TV, and we lived all squenched up above people, people on all sides so I couldn't move, and I got Sara to practice with me. You better not tangle with her, boy. She's good. A few times when we had the money, we went to see it live. Maybe we could practice some at recesses. We used to do it in the gym where I went to school."

121

"What's this I hear about a fight?" Miss Day asked before they were more than halfway across the porch. "How come you boys can't make it all the way to school without fussing?" When no one answered, she went on. "Si Brown and John Henry McCoy, you been fighting?"

John Henry looked up at Miss Day. She was walking so near him he could smell her perfume, apple blossoms. He didn't want to fib and he didn't want her to be angry. "We were wrestling," he said.

When there were several laughs and groans, she said, "Silas Brown, what have you got to say about this?"

"He showed me how he could wrestle. And it wasn't on school ground. Me and John Henry—"

"John Henry and I, Si. Si, it was John Henry and I."

Si rolled his eyes at John Henry. "You was in the house, Miss Day. It was me and John Henry a-wrestling, and he's a pretty good hand at it."

"All right, I'll take your word for it. Now, let's see if we can find anything else you boys are good at." She walked back to her desk and sat down and turned a stack of papers. "Writing, for instance."

She kept her eyes on them. She made Si do a page of writing over, and kept John Henry writing

122

by fours to a hundred. This was a little slow, since he had to figure them out in his head by adding fours as he went along.

At lunchtime, Si shared a bag of peanuts with him as they walked around trying to find a quiet place. Boys kept following and saying, "Fight," or, "You better not fight."

"You see us fight, you have to pay," Si told them. He whispered to John Henry, "Why don't we practice up and have a real fighting match and charge them to see it?" The boys left, and Si continued, "Practice at Grandad's store. Basement down under. He'll be so glad when he knows you're my friend, he won't charge us nothing for the basement. Maybe clean it out for him. You are my friend, aren't you?" John Henry didn't know what to say. "I mean, you see, I want you for my friend. I can't stand a sissy, goody that's more like a girl than a boy. Boys here, don't none of them like me because I'm tougher than they are, and because when they get behind at the store Grandad cuts their credit off."

"I don't know." John Henry needed time to think about this. It was moving from one direction to the other a little too quickly.

A big boy stepped from behind the schoolhouse.

"Si Brown got it poured on him. Now he has to buddy up," he said.

"One thing, I'm not buddying with you," Si said.

They moved to a whitewashed rock in front of the coal house, and Si talked like a creek in flood, explaining how the students expected him to fight since he whipped a new boy in first grade, and if he didn't start the fight they kept on talking until they started it. Fighting was the thing he could do best. And he liked being a champion, and he didn't like giving up that title, except to his friend John Henry. And he wanted John Henry to be his friend. John Henry agreed, and they planned their meetings for practice, for cleaning the basement and for making signs.

"We'll go hunting and fishing and all kinds of things," Si planned, and John Henry nodded.

The minute he got home, his mother said, "John Henry, I do wish you'd learn to stop at the post office."

"I've got to go back anyway, promised I would." Then he tried to explain about getting ready for the wrestling match. He called, "Here, Fido," over and over as he got his chores finished in a hurry.

124

"No mail," Mr. Thompson said when John Henry asked.

Every day there was no mail meant another day he could stay put and another day for him to stop being a stranger. While waiting for Si, he sat on a hay bale and watched Mr. Thompson whittle. He and Si practiced wrestling for about ten minutes and carried out paper and boxes and bottles for nearly a half hour. Along the creek bank, under the store, they found a four-leaf clover and three stones with fern imprints in them. John Henry offered to let Si have them, but Si had no use for them.

"I keep baseball cards's all," Si said. "And I'll be on the lookout for rocks and stuff for you if you'll watch for baseball cards for me. Oh, yes, I forgot. I keep coupons from writing-tablet covers and the cards that come in some candy."

On Friday morning, Granny started taking a cold. By the time John Henry and Sara returned from school, her cold was worse, and John Henry built a fire to take the chill from the house. When he returned from fight practice and the post office, she was in bed with a jar of warm water at her feet and three quilts wrapped about her. He brought a

125

catalog that said Box Holder and a letter from his father.

The letter said: "Dear wife Mary, Ma, and all, got a house spotted. You watch for another letter real soon. This is a fine job, and I think it'll last."

John Henry had the sad feeling that had been with him many times. He loved his father and missed him and wanted to hear from him, but he didn't want that next letter, not if it meant moving to a job that was fine and was supposed to last, not if it meant never staying put, always being new. Now it would mean leaving Si Brown. Si might not be the best friend anybody in the whole world had, but he was the best one John Henry had at the time, maybe the best one he'd ever had. Si wasn't bad at all, once the fight was over. The thing that worried John Henry most was that maybe Si was being too good, that it wouldn't last. And John Henry meant to make more friends, lots of them if he stayed here. He couldn't leave Miss Day and Fido.

"Oh," he groaned. Then he wished a wish he meant and didn't mean, and it made him very upset: "I wish we wouldn't hear from Daddy." To stop the bad feeling inside, he added, "About the house." Then he said, "I wish he didn't have that old job." But they had lived for a while without a job, and it wasn't something to wish, willingly, upon the family. For the family he went on, "That old job up there."

The next day Granny sat up for a while and put two pockets on the new shirt so it wouldn't be like the other one that had one pocket. Mrs. McCoy tore some old clothes into quilt scraps and rug strings. John Henry and Sara braided some of the strings. When Mrs. McCoy grew tired, she turned through the catalog and talked of styles she had known and dresses she had worn. John Henry pinned the end of the braid to the side of a mattress and left Sara to continue braiding by herself. He walked outside, around the house, calling, "Here, Fido. Here, good doggie." He ran his hands over some apple slices on a piece of tin, took up a slice and bit into it. It tasted like a piece of old sponge or rotten wood might taste, and he couldn't imagine why Granny had kept them all working so hard at the apples.

Clarabell tiptoed up behind him. "Who's Fido?"

"Nobody."

"I saw a dog today."

127

"Where?"

"Up the hill there." She pointed.

"If you see it tomorrow, will you call it and give it some bread?"

"We can't have a dog in town." Clarabell pointed to a willow tree. "Get some limbs and make us a jump rope. Granny told about it today, how you tie the limbs."

"We don't live in town," John Henry said a little sharply. He was sorry immediately, and he patted Clarabell's head. "We live right here in Hatfield Branch, at least for the time being. And you'll help me get Fido, won't you?"

While he broke some small branches from a willow and tied them for jump ropes, he talked about how nice a dog could be. "And especially to keep you company while we're at school, till your own Head Start begins."

They jumped until they were tired and went in for water.

Granny was sitting up in bed. "Too much cold in my eyes to do any sewing," she complained, "and me with sewing to do. Willow tea's suppose to be good for a cold, I just remember. Why don't you get some and make me up some tea?"

128

John Henry gathered willow branches and peeled the bark into small slabs. Sara rinsed the bark, and Mrs. McCoy set the pot of water and bark to boiling.

While Granny sipped the bitter, hot tea, which they had all tasted, she said, "I got a few right pretty quilts I'd let the Thompsons have on our charges and for some bread money." Clarabell got her quilt scrap bag and smoothed a finished square of red and black, a Bow Tie. Granny said, "When I get some things finished up, I'll have money to spruce up things with curtains and new paper for the front room and kitchen and maybe a little trim paint for the house, come spring." She wiped scissors on her apron tail. "Was a pattern my ma made once, I'd like to try my hand at, if I can remember how it goes. Road to Jerusalem."

John Henry froze at the word "road." He knew Granny was talking of a quilt pattern. But a road went away, a road took you off. When the time was ripe, he would ask the Thompsons about their need for quilts. He was so busy he hardly heard Granny's voice going on, naming the different colors she had used in Flower Gardens and Bear Paws and Kittens in Baskets. "Red and yellow makes the prettiest

Tulips, don't you think, Mary?" Granny asked. "If we had a good market for them, all of us working together could turn into a pretty fair quilt factory. Maybe Henry could look around up there for us."

"Henry'll be expecting us to go with him," Mrs. McCoy said.

Granny said, "I'm not so helpless I can't do something on my own. I'm going to stay put right here in this house. It's kind of like a dream come true, a house so big and fine. A little paint and paper and it'll be finer than some houses rent for a hundred dollars in town. I wouldn't be the first woman who stayed while her family went off to a job. Mary, you remember right down below us on Cow Creek a woman stayed right by herself, except for weekends when they come back?"

Mrs. McCoy studied the ends of her fingers, one at a time, before saying, "But you never did. We'd be lost without you, and one of the younguns'd have to stay to help you. And I can't figure out why you're suddenly so set on not going along with the family."

"Because I never did's no sign I never thought about it. I never had a good house like this before, and it'd be more settled for us all, you see. You

130

could all come back ever so often and visit. Could move back in, come a spell between jobs. And John Henry likes it here. He could stay with me, and we might round up a job later for Henry, if he wants to come back and stay. Way I see it, it'd be much better'n anything we've done in quite a while. That is, if it suits John Henry here."

John Henry nodded. He liked what Granny said. It had a good stay put, put down roots and be friends kind of sound, even if it meant the rest of the family would be away. Oh, he would miss them, and sometimes he might wish he had gone and that he had persuaded Granny to go. But even while he wished it, he'd be glad to have the solid ground under his feet and a friend and a dog and a lot of things and a place to keep those things. Even if it meant he had to work harder, if he had to set up a market for Granny's quilts. Maybe his father and mother would agree on letting him stay with Granny, if he begged long enough and hard enough.

Eight

On Wednesday evening, John Henry sat down on a bale of hay across from Mr. Thompson and rested and waited as long as he could before asking, "Any mail for us?" He was hoping Mr. Thompson would shake his head.

Mr. Thompson groaned. "Why didn't you ask while I was in there?" He got up, went to the little dark corner in the back of the store and reached into a box. "Letter from your pa, looks like." Mr. Thompson's brown corduroy pants went scratch, scram, scratch, scram as they rubbed together. "Couple of weeks from now we're going to have a cane patch ready. Work might be too hard for you and the womenfolks, if you're not real work-brickle. But I sure could use some help."

On the porch, Mr. Thompson gave John Henry the small envelope. John Henry stood holding it and wishing it could somehow disappear.

"You-all think about it. Could settle up what your Granny's traded, and be some molasses in the bargain. Indians called it long sweetening. Be something good to sop biscuits in all winter. Real good to cook with, dried apples and things. If you-all can help, you let me know before I get somebody else, hear?"

"We will. And good-by, Mr. Thompson," John Henry said.

If he had some way of opening the letter, he could change what it said. He stuck it carelessly in his back pocket. Maybe it would drop into the creek and wash away. Then he would have a week or so more, for certain. Nothing was certain now, nothing settled. His family talked one way and another, as

133

they always did. At the last minute, his father always decided what they would do.

He forgot everything else when he found the snakeskin beside a stump. It was long and thin and shiny. He carefully lifted and carried it on a stick, loose and dangling like a belt.

"What in the world's that?" his mother said.

"Get that thing away from here," Sara said.

"I'm putting it upstairs with my other things, and you don't go throwing it out."

"He's a pack rat, a plain old pack rat," Sara said. "He's brought in a hornet's nest and all kinds of junk."

"And you better leave it alone," he growled.

"Or what?" Sara asked.

"Or I'll throw out that rat's nest of dolls you've been cutting from catalogs and things."

Sara glared at him. "You just dare!"

He glared back at her. "And you just dare!"

"Stop that fussing, both of you. Any mail, son?" Mrs. McCoy asked.

"Letter from Daddy."

There was a special little ceremony each time a letter came. Mrs. McCoy took the letter, studied the front of it, turned it over, examined the back, held

134

it up to see which end could be torn without damaging the contents. Then she pinched off small pieces of the envelope. When the opening was complete, she withdrew the letter, unfolded and smoothed it with her hands.

"Looks like he didn't have much to write," she said before giving the letter to John Henry for reading aloud.

John Henry always knew there wouldn't be much writing on the page. His father had not learned to write very well. Letters were difficult for him, and he had told them many times, "You have to read between the lines."

"Go on. What're you waiting on?" Mrs. McCoy asked impatiently.

Granny leaned forward, as if she would take the letter and get the waiting over, even though she could read only a dozen or so words. Then, to give them privacy for the event, she said, "I'm thirsty" and went into the house.

"Dear wife Mary, Ma, and all, I will be sending money tomorrow for bus fare. Lock up things. I got a promise of a furnished house. Be ready when you get the money. I miss you all." John Henry read slowly, for he had to guess at some words.

Granny sneezed and groaned. John Henry went to see about her, carrying the letter. He read it to her before saying, "Your cold worse, Granny?"

She sat at the table, ran a forefinger over the oilcloth. "Taking a back set, I guess. Think maybe I'd best get in bed."

"We don't have a lock," Mrs. McCoy said as she came to the kitchen. She took the letter. "Maybe Mr. Thompson has locks. Granny, you want anything?"

When Granny shivered, Mrs. McCoy led her to bed, covered her up with a heavy quilt. The shivering stopped after a while and Granny said, "Mary, you honestly think Mr. Thompson'd let us lock up his house and not pay him rent on it? You think we can pay rent on two houses? Mary? Mary, answer me."

"Granny, you rest awhile."

John Henry said, "Mommy, I think we'll get on our feet better to stay here."

"What's that supposed to mean?"

"I don't want to move." He shuffled his feet over the floor, ran one toe up and down a small crack. "This is the best house we ever had, since I can remember anyway. Mr. Thompson rented it to

Granny free for the winter if we'd stay, remember? Can't we not move? We've moved and moved. Clarabell can go to Head Start if we stay."

"This last move was yours and Granny's, you know," Mrs. McCoy said.

"Head Start," Clarabell said. "I'll go."

"And I thought you liked the house, thought you liked all these rooms and the buildings outside and the garden and all. And we've got a good school." He wanted a definite answer.

Sara groaned. "It's not all that good, and you know it. Bucket water and outside restrooms and no playground things and no lunch room and no—"

Clarabell asked, "And no. What's that?"

"It is so good," John Henry said to Sara. "And I've got me a friend." He patted Clarabell's hand, which was reaching for the lamp Mrs. McCoy was lighting. "And no electricity here. You could think of some things we won't have if we move to Columbus."

Sara covered her mouth and patted a yawn. "I don't know what you mean. We could go to movies and things up there."

"And have no yard to play in, maybe, and no big apple trees, and all have to pile into one room or two

137

and can't even walk without tiptoeing, for people under us. Or we could be in a damp basement and listen to water running all night, and right next to a furnace and get woke up every time somebody puts in coal. Have to smell everything everybody's cooking and—" This wasn't it, really. He didn't know how to say exactly what he meant—that he didn't like the closeness of an apartment which never became home and people who moved in and out and never became friends. "Oh," he said wearily, "you wouldn't understand."

"Try again," Sara said.

"It's roots and stay-putness and settling down and—"

"It's all that, John Henry," Granny said. "And being tired and wanting to keep something to call your own and having a place of your own to put it."

"Si Brown's just another boy, and I wouldn't have him for a friend of mine on a Christmas tree," Sara snorted.

"And you with big plans for a room upstairs." John Henry rolled his eyes.

"You stop making faces at me. I can change my mind."

"You can, you surely can. And Si's a good friend, and don't you say he's not, and I've got me a pet."

"Pet?" Sara laughed. "I've not seen a living thing could be called a pet."

"Like I've got a dog when I find him."

Clarabell clapped her hand over her mouth and said "ooohh" as she removed it. "He's out in the smokehouse, John Henry. I put some bread, and he went in to get it, and I fastened him up."

John Henry couldn't wait another minute. He ran to the smokehouse, and there was the dog— Fido. Clarabell held the door while he knelt and patted the dog. "Come on, boy. Come on, puppy. My good dog."

Could he leave the dog? They couldn't ask him to do that! Could he cancel the fight planned for next Friday? Could he leave Si? Leave his rocks and nests and— he closed his eyes and rocked back and forth on his heels. Next week they would be subtracting in arithmetic, and Miss Day would straighten him out on it. She would teach him how to borrow. He put his head against the dog's side. Tears came, and he did not try to stop them.

"I declare supper's cold as an iron wedge," his mother called.

"Can I claim him for mine some, John Henry, for getting him?" Clarabell asked.

She put a sack in a box and made a bed for Fido.

"Sleep good here," she said as they went out. The dog whined at the door, then they heard him climbing into the box.

"Whooa," Mrs. McCoy said. "Wash real good. Use soap."

"I don't want anything," John Henry said.

"Everything looks better and feels better on a full stomach," Mrs. McCoy said.

He knew his mother was right. If he went to bed with an empty stomach he wouldn't be able to sleep. The potatoes were like stones. The glass of water was warm and choked him. The bread turned to ashes and stuck to the roof of his mouth. He forced a few bites down.

"If I ever live in the country again, I'm going to have me some chickens, raise my own eggs and have yellow gravy and fat dumplings and fryers," Mrs. McCoy said. "I hear a rooster every morning, from away off. It just don't seem like day unless you've got your own rooster to tell it's coming, and to parade around like a king, but I guess that'll have to wait awhile yet."

Sara took a second helping of potatoes. "I heard Mr. Thompson tell a woman the other day he had chickens for sale. She had some to trade, and he

140

said he had more chickens than he knew what to do with, and the price down."

"Price'll probably up when he sells them. Couldn't buy them anyway." Mrs. McCoy began scraping plates. "What would we do with chickens in a furnished apartment?"

"Right here, we could have feathers for stuffing these flabby old pillows and making more," Granny called from the bed where she was eating.

John Henry thought, "I'll buy them. We wouldn't go off and leave chickens, not a patch of real live chickens."

He took off early the next morning. Mr. Thompson had six hens he had taken in trade and didn't want to have to haul to town for selling. John Henry promised that he would pay three dollars for them soon, or he would work the cane for a week to pay for them. Mr. Thompson threw down corn for the hens, pointed out the ones for John Henry to catch and John Henry chased them down, one by one. Mr. Thompson tied their horny feet together.

"Know anybody's lost a dog?" John Henry asked.

"Can't say I do. Why?"

"Well, there's been a spotted one up our way for

a while. You think it's all right if I claim him?"

"Don't know why not. If he'd belonged to anybody around here they'd a found him before now. Lots of folks get rid of dogs by dumping them out around here. I'd say it's probably one somebody dumped. Two or three real good dogs come around here every year. When I find one, I tie him up for a spell, say about a month, and charge board bill if anybody claims him. If nobody don't, why then I sell him. How long's that dog been up there?"

John Henry rubbed the jagged red comb of a hen and hedged a little with Mr. Thompson. "He's been there a good spell."

"That wouldn't be a bluetick hound, would it? I've seen one around for a month or so, but he's kinda wild and takes off." Mr. Thompson rubbed his hands together when John Henry nodded. "Hmmm, now you wouldn't want to trade some more, would you? You let me have that hound, bring him in ready to tie up, and we'll call it even on the chickens?"

Sell Fido? For a minute he almost hated Mr. Thompson. To sell Fido would be like—why, it would be like selling himself! He tried to push the feeling away and think clearly. His mother would be pleased with the deal, and think him a fine trader. Maybe Granny would rather be in debt for the chickens, and maybe not. Sara wouldn't care one way or the other, since Fido was his dog and the chickens were his debt. But Clarabell would miss Fido. Clarabell needed Fido for company when he and Sara were at school.

"No, thank you, Mr. Thompson. I'll work in the cane for the chickens," he said as firmly as his shaky voice would allow.

Then he set off home in a great hurry, two chickens in one hand and one in the other. They lay warm and still for a minute or two at a time. One would squawk and rise up, then another and another, but he held onto them. He set them in the chicken house, patted Fido, who had just returned from a trip in the hills, and said, "Now, you stay here." Fido did not understand, and he followed John Henry down the hollow, running ahead a little and waiting, standing with his head down when John Henry said, "Go back," then following when John Henry raced ahead.

"That's him?" Mr. Thompson asked. "You changed your mind and want to let me have him?" When John Henry shook his head, Mr. Thompson continued, "I might could add onto the chickens. Say, what you and Granny owe me?"

John Henry dropped his head. It would be nice to clear up Granny's debt, but he couldn't do it. "No sir, he's not for trade," he said at last. He took up the three chickens, and Fido walked along beside him as if he understood that he truly belonged to John Henry now.

His mother was standing in the door, looking down the hollow. "John Henry McCoy, what in the world do you mean? And you a-knowing we can't have chickens. You can just take them right back where you got them."

A hen cackled, and Granny called, "John Henry, let me see."

He took the three squawking hens to the bed. They reared up their heads and lost several feathers on the floor. Granny reached out and patted one of the hens, a reddish-brown one, and the hen lay its head on the bed and rolled it about.

Granny chuckled. "You take them to the chicken house, son. You know how to feed them, I guess. Set some water and peelings and scraps. Keep them fastened up for a few days, and they won't wander off." She blew her nose and sneezed. "I'm not going

to be able to go anywhere either for quite a spell, the way this cold's got me pinned up."

Mrs. McCoy stared at her sternly. "Now, Granny, you know we'll have to."

"I don't know any such thing. I know more about how I feel than you do, and I'm feeling mighty poorly. I couldn't set up on no bus, car neither, and you know it, and if you younguns are a-going to school you'd better be getting a ready on. Looks like we're going to have to wait and let Henry put that roofing on."

Sara and Clarabell had been chasing each other around the house. Sara panted, "Where's them hens going to lay eggs? Won't we need to build some nests?"

They carried grass and made a nest in a box before leaving for school.

Si was waiting, and John Henry told him about the letter and about hoping that he could stay with Granny if the others wanted to go to Columbus.

Si coughed and sneezed and grinned. "Couldn't you take a cold too? Take a cold too, John Henry. I don't want you going off to no city. We got too much to do. Why, we've got to fight, and we've got to go possum hunting. There's the molasses to make, and I've got two roosters that fight all the time. You come after him next Saturday, and I'll loan you one to get rid of him for a while. He's a banty. Way off up there where you live, you could make money raising banties."

"Is that right?"

"That's right." Si's sweater sleeves were rolled above his elbows, and they pushed his arms out, like wings spread for flying. "People's moved off so, and the rest of 'em are too lazy to hunt. I bet if you set your mind to it you could hunt and trap and make you some money. Eat the meat and sell the skins. Like the pioneers did."

"You'd have to take half," John Henry said.

Si shrugged. "I don't need it. My old man's superintendent up at the Big Pony Coal Company. Boy, does he make the money! And Grandad gives me money." Si picked up a stone, aimed it at a hollow in a tree, and missed. "Shucks to it, I'll even give you half of whatever Grandad hands out."

"You trying to buy me or something?" John Henry asked. Si was being too free with things. Was it because he still had to play big shot? "I'm not for sale, and I don't want your handouts." He watched as Si seemed to shrink a little. Si was not a

147

champion fighter now. If John Henry left, Si would be just a boy who'd been whipped. It was all tangled up like Granny's quilting thread. Si needed him here, needed him badly enough to try and hire him to stay, but Si would use that, too, for making himself feel important and for trying to make a slave of John Henry. He liked Si and wanted him for a friend, maybe for an always-best friend, but he wanted some other friends also. He felt he might have been a little harsh, and he put his arm around Si's shoulder.

All the rest of the day, they did not mention the possibility that John Henry might be leaving.

On Saturday morning, they went to sit on the creek bank behind the store. Si had helped himself to some crackers and lunch meat in the store. When a minnow swam smooth as a knife through the water, Si threw a piece of the meat, and the minnow disappeared.

"Don't waste it. Give it to Fido," John Henry said, patting the dog.

"Country dog's supposed to hunt their own meat, city boy," Si said.

"And what's that supposed to mean?" John Henry sat up very straight. "If you don't like my dog—"

"Aw, don't get your hackles up so. It didn't mean

a thing. Only don't worry about Fido, with all the wild things running loose. How about that cold I mentioned?" Si gave Fido the last of the meat, and Fido sniffed it warily, licked it, then let it drop to the ground. He walked to a dry, sandy spot, turned around and lay down.

"If I played off sick, I might have to stop playing and go anyway. And how'd we live?"

"You're not been hearing a word I said. Like Daniel Boone and the other pioneers. Hunt. Fish. I thought you already planned to stay. Why don't you make up your mind? You really want to stay?"

"Now, you know I want to stay," John Henry said gruffly. "But I'm not the boss. Daddy'll have the final say. Mommy sees all the sides and talks one way and another. Then she does what Daddy says. I think I'll tell Miss Day that I need a job. Come on. Let's go up where she boards."

Si shook his head. "Can't go right now. I got to run home awhile."

John Henry dreaded the thought of going alone. Even worse, he hated to ask for a favor. But if he had to do it, he could. "All right," he said a little sharply, "if I have to go by myself, I will."

The sun was behind him, and he tried stepping over his shadow. He pulled a milkweed pod from a

149

stalk at the edge of the road and released the little silk parachutes. He wasn't asking a favor: he would be doing Miss Day a favor, he decided at last. When this decision was made, he hurried up the road with Fido at his heels.

Miss Day boarded at the house across the road from the school. She was at a table on the front porch, marking papers and nibbling at a sandwich, and she smiled as John Henry explained his offer.

"Teachers always pay somebody to sweep floors and build fires in winter. If I have a little job or two like that to bring in a little spending money, I probably can stay with my Granny and go to school here all year."

She measured him with her eyes. "You're sure you're big enough? It'll get mighty cold, and you'll have to be here early."

"I don't mind the cold," he said airily, as if he were an Eskimo. "Si Brown said that teachers paid ten cents for fires and ten cents for sweeping. I'd be awfully glad to do the work for you."

"All right, the job's yours, John Henry, and I do hope you can stay."

Halfway across the yard, he remembered to call back, "Thank you, Miss Day."

When John Henry got to the store Si was waiting, sitting on a hay bale with Mr. Thompson. "Got me a couple of little jobs with the teacher. You got anything I can work at, Mr. Thompson?" he asked at once.

Mr. Thompson was slower at answering. "Well, I don't know. You're in debt to me head over heels now." He kept on whittling, making curls of wood at his feet which looked something like Sara's hair when she pinned it up.

Si rocked the hay bale as he talked. "Grandad, he's going to help with the cane to pay for the chickens and things. What little bitty job could he have for everyday? You're always saying you got more'n you can do."

Si got up, and Mr. Thompson slapped the seat of his pants. John Henry turned to pat Fido, and Mr. Thompson slapped the seat of his pants also. "Not many boys want jobs. They just want the pay. When I pay for a job, I have to have the job done first. Does it mean that much to you boys?"

John Henry nodded, and Si said, "It does. He's the best buddy I ever had. He's the only real buddy I ever had."

"Is that so?" Mr. Thompson ran his fingers over

151

the piece of wood. "And you're my only grandson, Silas Hatfield Brown, and John Henry seems like a right good boy."

"You got all that name, big as mine?" John Henry said.

Si licked his lips and nodded. "One reason I learned to fight. Or tried to. And these buck teeth. When I got started fighting, everybody sort of egged me on. Now people tell their younguns, 'Stay away from that Si. He's a bad egg.'"

"Not been anybody really dug any ginseng or may apple in these parts for years. Ginseng pays big money. Maybe you ought to try that, come spring," Mr. Thompson said.

Si picked up a soft-drink bottle and carried it to a case. "A job, Grandad? A job?"

"Feed the pigs and horses evenings. Ten cents a day."

"They can't live on that, and you know it. Stingy," Si teased. "People used to say, 'Hezzy Thompson'd skin a gnat for its tallow.' And I'd get mad. They'd say, 'Hezzy Thompson sells his thumb every time he weighs anything,' and 'Hezzy Thompson squeezes a nickel till it turns green,' and I'd get madder."

152

Mr. Thompson shook his head and frowned at Si. "You boys get out'n my hair. He could make a few cents every once in a while rounding up pop bottles—and not the ones already here."

"Granny's got some quilts she'd like to sell," John Henry said.

"The old woman might be interested."

"How much for a quilt?" John Henry hated to sound like money was all he thought about, like he didn't appreciate what Mr. Thompson had already done, but they couldn't live without some food and heat.

"Why don't you ask her?"

John Henry had to clear up something. "If Mommy and Sara and Clarabell go off, will you let just me and Granny rent the house? Granny likes that place a sight, Mr. Thompson. Next year she wants a garden."

Mr. Thompson combed back his hair with his fingers. "Like I said before, I'd rather have somebody in the place. And seeing you're my friend, I'm renting it to just you and Granny right here and now. Now the way I look at it, if you're going to earn fifteen cents, you'd better be at that feeding job, and you could throw in a little barn cleaning

153

once in a while. Si here's too lazy to strike a tap at a snake. He could do these jobs for his old grandad. He can at least show you where's the feed and all."

They got the slop bucket from the back door and emptied it in a trough outside the barn-lot fence. Three small, sharp-backed hogs gobbled down the potato peelings and bread scraps at once. They gave a lard pail of chopped corn to the two plump, curly-tailed hogs in a pen, then gave them three large pails of water. They threw down four bundles of corn tops for the horse and the cow. And it was not work at all; it was fun, hiding in the stalls and throwing corn at each other, which Si said would feed the chickens at the same time.

Si's grandmother, Mammaw Thompson, was a plump, pleasant-faced woman with stiff fingers and large ankles. She listened and smoothed the ruffle on the edge of her apron while John Henry asked about the quilts.

Before she could answer, Si said, "He's my best pal, Mammaw, and they need the money. How much could you give?"

Mrs. Thompson rubbed her fingers one at a time before speaking. "Five dollars tacked and ten dollars new and fancy."

154

John Henry dropped his head. Granny had sold one in Cincinnati for thirty dollars. If they had the quilts in a city somewhere, they might sell them for forty or fifty dollars now. But the quilts were not in the city. The Thompsons would buy cheaply or not at all. After the days and days of work Granny had put into the house, she might not mind letting them have the quilts for a small price. And she might not like the price at all. Granny liked to feel she was getting a bargain, in one way or another.

Si groaned. "Mammaw! You're worse than Grandad. To ask anybody to work a week or two for five dollars. You can do better'n that. Say two fancy and new and one heavy tacked, how much? Me and John Henry can carry them to you tomorrow, if Granny'll agree, and they don't go on store bills. The store bill's his daddy's debt, see. This is for John Henry and Granny to live on. How about fifteen and ten?" Si winked at John Henry and licked his front teeth, letting his tongue fold and rest for a while in the gap between his teeth. "That'd be forty dollars, Mammaw, and they could eat right saving a month on that. And you might want to buy some for Christmas presents, you know that? Mama'd like some, I know."

155

Mrs. Thompson smiled. "You are a corker, a pure sight. And your Mammaw's favorite boy. But I'll have to see how good they are before I promise any Christmas presents, and you don't run to your mama and promise no quilts, you hear? I bet you boys wouldn't like to have a bite to eat, would you?"

She cut two slices of cornbread from an iron skillet on the great white stove and carried a saucer of soft fresh butter to the kitchen table.

Si took up his bread and dipped it into the butter. John Henry followed. He bit into the crisp crust dripping with butter, and he had never tasted anything so good in all his life.

He smacked his lips. "Mmmm, that's good, Mrs. Thompson."

"If you're going to be my boy, you'll have to call me Mammaw."

"Yes mam. Si calls my Granny Granny, and he's not even met her."

"I'm going to tomorrow, remember? I'll come up, and we'll bring down the quilts."

Si sounded as if the quilts were already sold. John Henry was not as certain about them. He waited until the bread and butter had vanished and Si was chasing a crumb across the table, flipping it, waiting, then flipping it again. He said, "Mammaw, my granny tells about use-to-be that people would let you borrow cows. And you could keep all the milk and butter and you paid back the baby calves. Does anybody still do that? I mean, do you know anybody who'd loan a cow? I think I could live on bread and butter."

"Have to have some other things for your health. Want some more?"

John Henry said he was full, just to be polite. But Si asked for more for both of them.

While they ate, Mrs. Thompson said, "There's a man down the road has some cows he might loan out, a Carl Johnson. He used to, I know. You'd have to talk to him about it, after you see what your family thinks."

John Henry knew what his granny would think: She would think it was great. She could make butter and clabber and cottage cheese and sweet milk, like when she was a girl. His mother would say, "We can't move a cow around, and you know it. Get used to one and have to move off and give her back." Sara and Clarabell would shout with joy and then forget all about it.

Si jumped so high he touched the big light hang-

157

ing from the ceiling. "Whooppee!" he shouted.

They chased each other around the house and laughed until they were so tired they fell over on the grass and rested. Then Si tried to make a sneak attack and pin John Henry to the mat of grass. John Henry jiggled until Si was on his knees, then he bucked Si to the ground.

John Henry wanted to pretend this was his way of life. He wanted to pretend he had everything settled, and he was a renter and a trader and a worker and a borrower. But his father would have the last word on that. They went to the basement and moved a sack of potatoes and a churn of pickled corn to a far corner. The basement was ready now for the big match. They were ready for it also. If John Henry didn't move.

Mrs. Thompson called, "Telephone, Si. It's your mama."

"Don't go away," Si said. "I'll be right back."

Nine

John Henry knew he had to go home. He had to ask
Mr. Thompson about the mail.

"Yep, it looks like another letter from your pa.
Awful thick. He wouldn't send out money, like that,
would he?"

John Henry shrugged in answer. "Thanks, Mr.
Thompson, and bye now, Si." To prove he was not
worried at all, he thumped Si and added, "You old

159

son of a gun. Here, Fido," he called. The dog had wandered off. This was the first time he had left Fido to do as he pleased. Maybe Fido didn't really want to stay with him. Maybe Fido knew when he had been forgotten!

Si ran after John Henry and thumped him on the back. John Henry thumped Si again. They kept this up until John Henry was halfway up the hollow and it was getting too dark for seeing anything.

"They're going to take my hide and hang it up to dry for being out this late," Si said. "See you tomorrow."

When Mr. Thompson gave him the letter, John Henry had felt empty inside. Now the emptiness was filled. He was heavy as a stone. If there was water enough and he stepped into it, he would drown. He stopped so suddenly he nearly fell. He couldn't, he wouldn't, he shouldn't leave Si and Fido and the chickens and his turtle shell and snakeskin, and everything.

There was a light ahead, a low, three-cornered yellowish light coming from the kitchen window. He remembered the letter and patted his left hip pocket. It was empty! He patted the other pockets, all of them, and they were empty, except for two

160

marbles, a rubber band, a buckeye, a fern-imprinted piece of coal and a bent nail that Si had said was a good-luck piece. He couldn't find the letter in the dark, and he couldn't go home without it. He was supposed to be taking care of the family! Out horsing around. He was so ashamed he could die.

Then Fido was there, licking his hands, slapping with his tail, talking in low grunts and whines. John Henry sat down and hugged the dog to him.

Someone was shaking him. Sara. There was a light in his eyes. His mother was holding a lamp and saying, "How could you do this? John Henry Mc-Coy, how could you worry me like this, and me with no telephone? I never wanted a telephone so bad in all my life." She was crying, and the words were coming out one at a time, like chopped-up first-grade reading. "And no police to call. How could you lay out like this? Young man—"

Sara took over. "Mommy's been walking the floor, and I've been shouting my head off, and close as you are, you could've answered. Leaving me them old chickens to feed and all the work to do. You're big enough to know better."

John Henry knew how they felt. Once Clarabell

had run across the street and narrowly escaped being hit by a car. He had been so happy that she was safe that he didn't quite know how to say it. He had fussed at her for frightening him and for not minding.

Fido stood looking on, his nose pointing downward, as if he were ashamed.

"I went to sleep," John Henry said.

"But why? And you in sight of the house?"

"I got a letter from Daddy with money in it, and I lost it."

"You never? Oh, John Henry, you never?"

"I did, and I couldn't see to try and hunt for it in the dark."

Lamp close to the ground, Mrs. McCoy led the way along the creek bank. And there was the letter, in about the same spot where he gave Si the last thump on the back.

Mrs. McCoy gave Sara the lamp to hold while she shook John Henry. "I ought to beat the tar out'n you. Just for this, I ought to—" When he sneezed, she put her arm around him and said, "Oh, son, I hope you don't take a cold over all this."

Sara carried the lamp ahead of them, holding it low so they could step on smooth dry ground.

"You like it here, Mommy?" he asked.

"Well enough, I reckon, if we had electricity and a phone."

"Mr. Thompson's got a phone. Maybe we can get them to put one in for what that trip to Columbus'd cost."

"We might could," she said.

"And we wouldn't stay up there but a little while till Daddy'd be laid off or something, and we'd be a-needing to come back, and Mr. Thompson wouldn't let us have this place again."

She stopped at the porch to let him step ahead of her. She slapped the wet seat of his pants. "I'm not married to this place. Home's wherever my family is, and your daddy's still boss."

They were walking across the porch, and Granny answered, "I've heard the Eskimos used to leave their old people and move on. No snow yet, but it'll come, and I'm not moving a foot out of this place."

They walked through one of the empty bedrooms, their footsteps echoing strangely.

Mrs. McCoy scolded, "Now, Granny, you don't talk foolishness like that. We've not even read the letter." She opened the envelope and pulled out two twenty-dollar bills and a ten, drew a deep breath and said, "We'll have to go. We can't desert Henry."

Her voice sounded a little sad, and he wished he could read the letter to suit himself and say: "Dear wife Mary, Ma, and all, I want you to stay where you are, and I'll come home soon." But he couldn't do that. It wouldn't be right, and it wouldn't be fair not to let everyone have a choice. He read, "Dear wife Mary, Ma, and all, thought I had us an apartment, but then they said no kids, but I'll have one by the time you get here on the bus."

Mrs. McCoy sat down heavily, sat silently, took the letter from John Henry and laid it on the table beside the bed. Granny coughed. John Henry sneezed. Clarabell stood up and began bouncing across Granny and back again.

Sara said, "Sit in a bus station, like we did one time? Stay there, like we're going somewhere, in and out, afraid the police'll get us? Mommy, let's wait till he gets us a place."

Mrs. McCoy said, "We can't take Granny out till her cold's better, and that's for sure."

Granny nodded. "Henry don't know about my cold. You'll have to let him know."

"I sure as shooting don't want to go without a

house, and I think I may not want to go at all. I've got me a friend now. Nancy wants me to spend next Friday night with her," Sara said.

Granny chuckled. "Sara's like a feather. She goes whichever way she thinks the wind's blowing." Then she patted Sara's hand. "It's a good way to be sometimes. When you can't fight something, sometimes the best thing to do's join up with it and then make whatever changes you can make to suit yourself."

John Henry had been too busy to notice that Sara had a friend. He remembered what she had said about Si: "Some friend," and he wanted to get even with her, but this was not the time to do it. While Sara was on his side, he'd better keep her there, he decided. "Why don't you-all call Daddy tomorrow and tell him how Granny is, and let me speak to him about us staying here? Daddy wants to do what's best for us, I know. He might pet himself just a speck and argue a little, but he'll agree when he really knows how it all is."

Mrs. McCoy wound the clock. "Might do better to take that money and buy us a sack of beans and some boots, pay a little on what we owe Mr. Thompson. If work stays good, rent we save will put in the electricity, come spring. And come spring, maybe we can get a telephone, if we still think we need one. Buy some seeds to plant. It's late and we'd better get some sleep. We'll call Henry tomorrow and lay it all before him and let him decide."

"Know something?" Granny said. "While you-all was gone, I remembered what that bottle up there might've been for. Under the window. Supposed to catch bad luck and keep it trapped. Supposed to bring good luck. Maybe we'd better put us another one up somewhere."

John Henry knew the gap was narrowing when he heard his mother say to Granny, "I've always wanted blue morning glory vines on a porch. You know, one month's rent up there'd buy seed enough for a big crop. Columbus is close enough till Henry can drive home every couple of weeks, at least, like he did for a while three years ago." One of her shoes hit the floor. "Don't let me forget to get us some sugar tomorrow so we can make us some mullein cough syrup. Get it when I go down to call Henry."

Tonight John Henry's hopes rode high as the

moon outside the window. Sinking into the warm
bed was something like a plant going into the earth.

Sara got her bobby pins and began making a row
of flat curls across her forehead. "I'm not a feather,
Granny. It's that I like friends. They say, 'You-all
come back, and you-all write,' and we say, 'We will,
and you-all come to see us.' And we never see them
again, and all that."

"I know," Granny answered.

Tomorrow if Granny didn't like the price the
Thompsons offered, she could refuse it and make
a trade with them later. He thought about the
bottle that had been under the window. It hadn't
brought luck to the people who lived there before
them, or had it? Blue morning glories on the porch.
Bees on clover. Arrowheads and turtle shells.

John Henry suddenly remembered his chores.
"Did anybody feed the chickens?"

"I did," Sara said. "Found two eggs."

Fido walked across the porch and lay down on
the sack Clarabell had placed there for him. A hen
sang, "Cut-a-cut." An owl hooted. John Henry lay
there thinking of the things they had collected.
Maybe they wouldn't be able to keep all of them,
but it was good to have them for now. He wiggled

168

his toes and thought about all the things he might have, given time and space. He thought about his school, his dog, his friends. It was a nice feeling, and he smiled as Granny's breathing told him she was already asleep.